TOM SWIFT™

young inventor

Don't Miss Tom's Next Adventures!

TOM SWIFT™

young inventor

#4 ROCKET RACERS

By Victor Appleton

Aladdin Paperbacks
New York London Toronto Sydney

This book is a work of fiction. Any references to historical events,
real people, or real locales are used fictitiously. Other names,
characters, places, and incidents are the product of the author's
imagination, and any resemblance to actual events or locales or
persons, living or dead, is entirely coincidental.

ALADDIN PAPERBACKS
An imprint of Simon & Schuster Children's Publishing Division
1230 Avenue of the Americas, New York, NY 10020
copyright © 2007 by Simon & Schuster, Inc.

Designed by Lisa Vega
The text of this book was set in Weiss.
Manufactured in the United States of America
First Aladdin Paperbacks edition January 2007
2 4 6 8 10 9 7 5 3 1

Library of Congress Control Number 2006926491
ISBN-13: 978-1-4169-3488-2
ISBN-10: 1-4169-3488-X

Contents

ROCKET RACERS

Test Flight

I hadn't expected turbulence at this low an altitude, but the way my Swift-Racer was bucking, I knew I was in for a bumpy race. I checked and rechecked my stabilizers, fired my afterburners again to make sure the fuel was reaching the engine of my rocket racers, and . . . *THWACK!* The joystick nearly jumped out of my grip.

I gritted my teeth together and grasped the joystick with both hands, struggling to keep the plane under control. The clouds were racing past the canopy of my aircraft too quickly. If I didn't get this puppy flying straight in less than a minute, it was going to be lights-out time.

There! There's the horizon. Level off. Reduce lift. The Swift-Racer started to behave. It wasn't turbulence

at all. It looked like it was a bad mixture of isopropyl-alcohol fuel going to my twin jet engines. Either that or the reciprocating piston pump I installed wasn't timing correctly. The last thing I needed was to feel that buck again, but I knew a hairpin turn was up ahead. I wasn't going to be able to come out of the turn with any speed while gliding.

I could see the preprogrammed trajectory my racer was to follow displayed on the visor of my helmet. Like a "flight tunnel," the blue triangles seemed to be waiting out in front of me, showing me where to bank, where to decrease elevation, and where to turn.

And at nearly 160 miles per hour, that sharp turn was coming up fast.

A siren went off inside the cockpit, followed by a very loud voice.

"Swift, you punk! Are you paying attention to your fuel gauge? Now drop and give me fifty! Do you understand?"

"Not now, Q.U.I.P.," I answered quickly, trying to keep calm. Q.U.I.P., also known as Quantum Utilizing Interactive Processor, is essentially a supercomputer that I can talk to via a chip on my wristwatch. It was one of my first forays into artificial intelligence and is always coming in handy when I need another brain. The initial concept was to create a super-intelligent personality that I could work with and would continue to learn the more we communicated. The first several prototypes were about as fun to interact with as the most boring advanced calculus professor you could think of. Don't get me wrong: I love advanced calculus as much as the next teenage inventor, but more often than not, advanced calculus *teachers* have the personality of a plate of cold French fries.

Fortunately my science teacher, Mr. Radnor, has more than enough personality to make up for most of the rest of the teaching staff at Shopton High. With a flair for the dramatic, Mr. Radnor is able to bring any topic to life. One semester, to explain photosynthesis and the effect sunlight has on plants, Mr. Radnor transplanted a dozen grapevines into the ground outside the science lab. When the grapes finally began growing, the vines were crawling into the lab windows. At the end of the semester, after we had picked all the grapes, he rolled up his pants' legs, washed his feet, and stomped on them in a wooden vat, just like they used to do in Italy to make wine. The juice was good, but the memory of him ankle deep in purple Concord grapes was even sweeter.

So when it came time to give Q.U.I.P. a personality, Mr. Radnor came immediately to mind. And since that time, I've toyed with various other personalities and accents to enhance the interactive experience.

From Cowboy mode to Sherlock Holmes mode to Arnold Schwarzenegger mode to my best friend Bud Barclay mode, even Bugs Bunny's Brooklyn accent—whenever I get bored, I just change the personality of the supercomputer. And right now I was regretting that I had left it on "Staff Sergeant." I took one hand off the joystick, clicked a button on the wrist device, and turned Q.U.I.P. off.

But the siren continued. Dang it! That was the last thing I needed.

The turn was coming up quick. Now or never. I gave the Swift-Racer all the fuel in her tanks and slammed the joystick into my left thigh to take the turn.

I never knew what hit me!

To my left a gash of flames tore through the metal skin of my rocket racer. The buck of the racer was so violent this time that my visor and helmet shook off. I was flying blind.

The explosion washed over the cockpit with such a fury that it was several moments before I was able to blink the flash out of my eyes. The instruments were going nuts! Elevation: plummeting. Fuel: nonexistent. Pitch: crazy.

Then I saw it. The left wing was hanging on by a scrap of metal. The blast tore through the hull of the racer, shredding the left engine rocket. All this, and my last drops of fuel were pouring out in yellow and red shrieks of fire from what was left of the engine.

"Dude." Bud Barclay's voice came on over the cockpit's intercom.

I hit Q.U.I.P. again with my hand. I must have made a mistake and switched to Bud Barclay mode instead of turning it off. Bud may be my best friend in the whole world, but the last thing I wanted to hear was his voice in my ear as my aircraft was quickly losing altitude while traveling 160 miles per hour.

"Dude." His voice again.

I tried to ignore it. Tried to get control of the joystick, which was jumping like a cricket on a hot rock. Tried to peer through the smoke. Tried, tried, tried.

"Dude!" he said even louder. "You're toast."

The instrument panel lit up brighter than Chinatown at Chinese New Year.

Maybe with a little patented Swift luck, I might chance into a gust of wind, or catch an updraft.

No luck. The ground was coming up faster than even I anticipated. I was picking up speed.

I knew the next thing I would see was the blacktop and then nothing.

"Tom!" Bud shouted.

With the prospect of plunging into the earth at over 160 miles per hour, I tore my hand from the joystick and punched at the canopy of my racer. Game over.

No noise. No anything.

I sat for a moment in my virtual-reality flight simulator and caught my breath. I tapped my wrist, turning Q.U.I.P. on.

"What happened?" I exhaled.

"You died," Q.U.I.P. responded. Its voice was back to normal, in Regular Guy mode.

"How?" I asked, slightly perturbed.

"You crashed."

I was losing my patience with this glorified wristwatch. I didn't regret inventing it, although perhaps I shouldn't have given it so much intelligence that it could have a laugh at my expense.

"Would you like to try again?" Q.U.I.P. asked.

"No," I replied. "I try to keep from dying more than once a day."

"That's a sound policy, flyboy," Bud interjected over the loudspeaker.

I removed the helmet and visor that had fallen to my feet during the "flight" and hoisted myself up out of the simulator's seat, rubbing my head where it had hit the cockpit's canopy. I walked out to find both Bud and my other best friend, Yolanda, rewatching my fiery death on their plasma-screen monitors.

"How'd those new shocks work out in the simulator?" Bud asked. "Lifelike enough for you?"

"Perhaps you'd like to go a round or two with them," I said. It was supposed to be funnier than it sounded, but I was still a little shaken from the race in the simulator.

With his feet propped up on the desk and his hands behind his head, Bud Barclay looked like an unfurled marionette at rest. In geometric terms, Bud is a collection of right angles for shoulders and elbows, two long and skinny tubes for legs, and a slender rectangle for a chest, topped by a buckyball for a head. The buckyball is also known as a 60-carbon atom buckminsterfullerene molecule. It was named after Buckminster Fuller, the creator of the geodesic dome, like Epcot Center at Walt Disney World. Fuller was an inventor who wanted to use science for the betterment of mankind, and a hero of mine.

Bud ran his fingers through his curly black hair and smiled.

"Look," he said. "Look here." He pointed at the plasma monitor. "Here's where your stabilizer-thingies kinda gave out."

Stabilizer-thingies! Bud's my head mechanic for the upcoming Junior Rocket Rally and he still didn't know the names of the parts of my aircraft! Book knowledge he has, common sense he has, a talent for getting to the bottom of things he has, but science is not his strong suit. I suppose I could have found a more qualified head mechanic, but I never could have found someone I trusted more. And with all the rumors over the Internet of possible sabotage at the Junior Rocket Rally, I felt I needed someone in my corner who wasn't a question mark.

Swift Enterprises has been bedeviled by antitechnology groups ever since my dad created the company, before I was born. The worst is TRB—The Road Back. They are so committed to returning the world back to its "natural state" that they will stop at nothing to achieve their goal. And it seems the more inventions we bring to the marketplace, the more they want to shut us down. But they've thrown everything they've had at us in the past and nothing's worked yet. My dad's motto is to never give in to their backward demands. Still, a dozen times a year they try to gum up Swift Enterprises with computer viruses. And the last thing I needed now was for my rocket racer's onboard computer to be crippled by a virus.

And that's where Yolanda Aponte came in. You wouldn't know it from her runner's build and her long hair, but on the inside, Yo is an übergeek. Nothing pleases her more than writing code, rewiring motherboards, and repairing CPUs. She can spot a computer virus a mile away and disable it before it does its damage. She is also becoming quite handy with a wrench. More than once when

Bud wasn't here, she could be found underneath the Swift-Racer, tweaking the fuel intake valve.

"You know," she said, clicking the top of her pen, "your S-Racer *was* in first place—"

"Before you crashed to your death, that is," Bud interrupted, holding up his right hand for a high five.

Yolanda stared at him.

"Yo, don't leave me hangin'," he mock-pleaded.

I shook off their shenanigans to go examine the real S-Racer.

"Swift, Thomas Jr.," I announced as I approached the door leading out of my laboratory.

"Will you be returning to the laboratory again this evening, Tom Swift?" the voice-enhanced security system called Lab-Sec asked from a speaker above the door.

"Not tonight," I answered. "But Bud and Yo are still here."

"Affirmative, Tom Swift," the pleasant-sounding female voice replied after a moment. "Yolanda Aponte is currently in the computer room accessing aeronautical flight design information from the Massachusetts Institute of Technology database via a satellite dish connection courtesy of a NASA security code." The security program paused as it accessed the whereabouts of Bud. "Bud Barclay is watching the Comedy Channel on television."

I rolled my eyes and exhaled. That would be Bud, always goofing off.

"Do me a favor, Lab-Sec. Change the channel he's watching to that *Giants of Applied Mathematics* show I recorded last week."

I waited a moment, and—like clock work—I heard Bud's booming voice: "Swift!"

Smiling, I turned toward the security system again.

"Lab-Sec, commence identification."

At once a retractable metal arm folded out of the wall near the door with a special retina scanner on it. I opened my eyes wide, and the light swept across my face.

"Confirmed," Lab-Sec said.

I then held out my open palm, and another metal arm reached from the wall with a small pencil-eraser-size temperature and body sweat chemical composition gauge on the end. It touched directly in the center of my hand. And after a moment of "reading" my palm, it retracted.

"Confirmed." A pause. "Tom Swift?"

"Yes, Lab-Sec?"

"Your temperature is higher than normal. Do you feel unwell?"

"No. I just died a few minutes ago in the flight simulator. I guess that raised my heart rate and temperature a few degrees."

"I'm sorry to hear you died, Tom Swift," Lab-Sec responded with no sincerity whatsoever. I had never intended the voice-enhanced security system to have a personality like Q.U.I.P.'s and so it was never able to learn either pathos or humor.

"Thank you, Lab-Sec."

"Favorite color?"

"Pistachio," I said. This was my attempt at humor. If someone had been able to trick the security system getting *into* the laboratory by somehow duplicating my physical components, they would never be able to get out. Because, try as they might to answer this question, they could never come up with the final key. You see, pistachio is my favorite ice cream flavor. It's a trick question. It doesn't really make any sense. And most people are going to think that all inventors are logical to a fault.

"Confirmed," Lab-Sec said, and the door before me opened.

The lights in the corridor that connect my laboratory to our family's house snapped on. It is a five-hundred-foot passageway from the laboratory that I had designed and installed in the hill behind the house so that I could work late at night and not have to ride my bike back home in the dark from Swift Enterprises on the edge of town. That was before I got my driver's license. But it still made sense to use it. I could roll out of bed in the middle of the night if I had a *Eureka!* moment and needed to sketch out a new invention. I passed through the door.

"Thanks, Lab-Sec."

"You're welcome, Tom Swift."

By the time I reached the garage, I had worked out a more appropriate isopropyl-alcohol fuel-burn ratio in conjunction with the speed the pistons were firing. It was a minor modification I could incorporate into the aircraft when we brought the rocket-powered Swift-Racer to the skytrack next week for time trials.

"Garage. Lights on," I said to the cognitive "smart house" technology my father and I wired into the house to obey our verbal commands. The light went on.

I walked over to where the S-Racer sat, its shiny wings peeking out from underneath a light brown cover. The metal was cold to my touch.

After the disaster in the flight simulator, I was more than a little apprehensive to get up in the air and fly against three other competitors for real. But I shook off the worries and decided that the best course of action would be to get some sleep and attack any problems in the morning with a clear head.

Then I felt the soft body of my sister Sandy's cat against my ankles.

"Hi, Emma," I said, bending over to pet it. I'm more of a dog person, but I do admit Emma is a friendly cat and a good pet. "How did you get in here?"

I saw the side door was open. "Come on, Emma. It's too warm a night to be in this stuffy garage." I picked up the cat and placed her outside. She meowed and scurried beneath a bush. I closed the door and made a mental note to wire the garage for security. We'd never had any problems with people sneaking into the house before, but I figured it couldn't hurt. I returned to the S-Racer. Nothing looked out of place.

"Garage. Lights out."

I stood for a moment in the darkness, feeling the coolness of the plane against my fingertips. Tomorrow was the maiden flight. I was essentially going to be strapping myself into a cockpit fixed on top of two powerful rockets fed by a highly volatile kerosene type fuel and praying for dear life that I could control the thing.

Should be interesting.

The Road to the Airport

Bud and I decided it was too nice a day not to have the top down on the Swift Speedster. Unfortunately Yolanda and my kid sister, Sandy, didn't see it that way.

"Tom!" they both shouted as I hit the button that retracts the roof. Instantly their hair took flight, blowing every which way but the direction they tried to smooth it. Yolanda reached into the knapsack she carried with her everywhere. It held her personal Swift-tronics laptop computer and a few other items. She pulled out a baseball cap and put it over her wavy dark hair. Time and again she complained that her nearly black hair was as easy to manage as an unstable free radical in organic chemistry.

She took off a thin black rubber gasket that she

wore as a bracelet and handed it to my sister. Sandy took it, grabbed her blond mane, and tied it up. Yolanda had already returned her attention to the Rocket Rally flight manual.

"If I get bugs in my teeth . . . ," Sandy shouted over the road noise.

"It might be an improvement," I shot back. Bud laughed with me. Kind of a guys versus girls thing.

"Hey, that's mature!" she said, and flicked me in the ear.

For just an instant I thought of turning up the radio and drowning her out. That really would have driven her nuts. Instead I replied coolly, "Would you like it if I turned around and went home? I'm sure I could find someone else for my rally pit crew."

I readjusted the mirror and saw her slouch back into her seat. She was steaming, but knew she had better not answer back in case I wasn't bluffing. Sandy had begged for weeks to be a member of my crew and I resisted the notion. Why? I guess because she always wants to be a part of what I'm doing. But, despite being an annoying younger sister at times, she does have some redeeming qualities. Take for example her ability to perform almost any type of mathematical equation in her head. I may have inherited Dad's love of inventing, but she got his computational smarts.

She gets her photographic memory from Mom. Together they try to stump each other with the most arcane trivia imaginable. Like the time they fought over who was the fourth person to reach the top of Mount Everest. Who knows this kind of stuff? My kid sister.

Needless to say, they were both correct. It was two men from the same climbing expedition.

But I hadn't seen how that type of talent was going to benefit me when I was in the cockpit of my Swift-Racer traveling at 160 miles per hour, 3,000 feet above the ground.

So she talked to Mom, and Mom talked to me, and before I knew it, I had my third pit crew member. I have to admit she has come in handy. Like when we were trying to figure out flight deviancy trajectories caused by rocket heat displacement over the wings. The computers at my lab were tied up analyzing wind tunnel data, so we asked Sandy.

Boom! Did she nail those trajectories! Sometimes down to four digits behind the decimal point.

But right now she wasn't a budding genius, she was my kid sister by a year. And she was pouting like she was a lot younger.

Bud looked from me to Sandy and back. "Tom Swift—point and match."

But I realized I was being crummy to Sandy and I was just about to apologize when Yolanda spoke up, waving the *Rules and Regulations* booklet.

"Tom, it says here that you'll only have one opportunity to refuel your aircraft. I thought they were gonna let you refuel at least twice." She took out a pencil and rubbed the eraser against her forehead. She does that a lot when she is thrown a whammy.

"Just been changed," I said easily, shifting gears and switching lanes. I was heading east on the highway. The rally was being held at the refurbished old airgrounds outside of Shopton. "C. J. was worried that the crowd would lose interest if the planes were on the ground too long between laps."

"Hold on," Bud shouted, grabbing his reporter's notebook and flipping to an empty page. He pulled out a pencil from behind his ear. Here was the *Shopton Gazette*'s ace beat reporter on the story. Not only does

Bud have a keen eye for a story, but he also has the distinct ability to craft and write a news piece, no matter how complicated, in a way the average reader can understand.

"Now, who is C. J.?" he asked.

"Carmen Juanita Garcia," I told him.

"But that throws off our glide and burn model," Yo protested, scribbling something in the margin of the *Rules and Regs* booklet. "The Swift-Racer will now have to glide almost four times longer than we allowed for."

"Three-point-seven," I corrected her. "Don't worry, I already compensated for the drag caused by lessening the propulsion time."

"Who is Carmen Juanita Garcia?" Bud asked.

"Bud, I thought we already went over this," I protested. "She's an old friend of the family. The Junior Rocket Rally is her idea. You remember: only teenage fliers."

"Yeah, yeah, yeah," Bud said, jotting down his notes.

"Did you factor in the drag coefficient in regards to the turn ratios?" Yo interrupted.

"To an extent. To be honest with you, I'm not quite

sure how the new airfoil design of the wings is going to perform," I said.

"What does she do?" Bud Barclay, the *bud*ding reporter queried me, no doubt gathering facts for his school newspaper exclusive.

"Didn't you do *any* research?" I asked.

"Research?!" he yelped. "When would I have time for research? School till three. Write, do interviews, and edit the *Shopton Gazette* till five. Run home, eat the quickest dinner known to man, and then sprint to your lab so I can learn how to be head mechanic in your pit crew. When do I have a moment to myself?"

"Right now," I shot back, and punched a button on the dashboard. The glove compartment door opened. Out slid a built-in Swift computer with a silicon-based chip capable of operating at frequencies above five hundred gigahertz. I was able to get that speed by cryogenically "freezing" the circuitry, using the special coolant Swift Enterprises had developed for the Speedster's air-conditioning. In a blink the Internet was up.

"Satellite wireless?" Bud asked, impressed.

"No doubt, beamed from the stars to you," I

replied. "Motherboard's in the trunk. I had Yolanda wire it up for me."

"Yo!" Bud shot out. "Sweet work!"

That's high praise from Bud Barclay. He reached back to Yolanda for a high five, but Yolanda was too immersed in her calculations to respond. In a moment, Bud was pounding away on the keyboard.

"All of the air tunnel tests we ran involved a high-speed airfoil with very little camber," Yo said, her eyes narrowed with thought.

"It says here," Bud said, not looking up from the computer, "that Carmen Garcia is a Texas entrepreneur who has sunk millions into turning that junk pit of an airport outside Shopton into a state-of-the-art facility for hosting rocket races." He whistled and repeated, "Millions."

"Remember the engine problems in relation to the wings that we were having?" I said to Yo. "I streamlined the profile, and the camber problem sort of solved itself. Plus, the polymer we covered the racer with will increase the laminar flow."

Bud looked up from the screen, puzzled. "Who is Laminar Flow?"

The commissary at the airport had been converted into a makeshift conference room. About two dozen reporters were sitting in plastic chairs, either drinking coffee or checking their e-mails on Blackberries. Bud and I entered the room and headed toward two empty seats in the back.

"Laminar flow is not a who, but a what," I started to explain to Bud as we sat down. He was already scribbling madly in his notebook, oblivious to the fact that Carmen Garcia was walking up to the platform.

After the perfunctory round of pictures, she stepped up to the podium. She was nicely dressed, I thought. Black skirt and tights topped with a leather flight jacket with the new logo of the Junior Rocket Rally emblazoned upon it. Her brown hair hung loosely down to the collar of her jacket, and small diamond earrings caught the light of the photographers' flashes. I had seen her numerous times at her ranch in jeans and a sweatshirt, and was taken slightly aback by how attractive she looked. No doubt she had a sizable investment riding on this race and wanted to get the best press and pictures she could.

"Ladies and gentleman," she began, "this is how it works."

Right to the point—that's one of the reasons she was my favorite of my parents' friends.

"The race will take place along a mile-long, three-dimensional 'racetrack' five thousand feet above the Earth—near enough so that spectators can follow, but not so near that they'll be singed by the exhaust these rocket racers spit out."

Carmen paused a moment for the reporters to take down the information, then continued.

"Global positioning units will define the invisible lanes for each plane to keep them from colliding with one another."

"Are you saying there's no chance of an in-air collision?" asked a skeptical reporter.

"None," C. J. shot back, and paused a moment before adding, "This isn't NASCAR."

A round of chuckles rose from the press corps.

"Kidding aside," she went on, "for safety's sake, all pilots will be required to stay in their own individual 'skylanes.'"

"Skylanes?" Bud piped up.

"That's right," Carmen said. "Above each pilot's

individual dashboard, on the glass canopy, there will be an illuminated projection of his or her 'flight tunnel.' Visual markers will display which route of the course each plane is to take. For example, Tom Swift's flight tunnel will be a series of blue triangles stretching out before him in the sky showing him where to turn, dip, and rise. Imagine, if you will, orange cones construction workers put on the highway. Sue Itami's flight tunnel will comprise of green stars, Karim al-Misri's will be red circles, and Andy Foger's route will be marked off by maroon squares."

Karim al-Misri, I thought to myself. I hadn't met him yet, although I had read a little about him on the Internet. Sue I knew from the Robot Olympics. Andy Foger I knew all too well. You might classify him as an insecure jerk with an inflated sense of himself. And that's his good side.

"Let me continue," Carmen said, grasping the top of the podium with both hands. "The race will only last about thirty minutes. Since each plane carries only about four minutes' worth of rocket fuel, the test will not be who can go the fastest, but instead who can time his or her boosters so that there is the proper balance of fuel burn and glide."

"Burn and glide," Bud murmured, still furiously taking notes.

"Knowing when and how long to fire the boosters will play a big part in determining who finishes the race first, and"—Carmen paused again—"who finishes last."

Several reporters' arms shot up to ask more questions, but C. J. waved them aside.

"I'm sorry, everyone, this has to be the end of the news conference. I'd like to see the pilots out on the tarmac."

There was scattered applause as everyone rose to leave.

"I don't have to tell you how important this race is, do I, pilots?" C. J. asked rhetorically.

We were all standing out on the tarmac that had recently been reblacktopped thanks to C. J.'s investment in this airfield and the Rocket Rally. The smell of tar was fresh, and the sun was rising to its full strength. I thought that C. J. must be pretty warm underneath her leather jacket. But if she was, she wasn't showing it. All business, cool and collected.

"We are going to show the world that rocket rally racing is a viable sport—not only safe but fun to watch, as well," she said briskly. "Denny?"

A slight, nerdy man in his mid-thirties had been standing silently behind us. Now, with a wide gait, he walked around the gaggle of pilots and approached C. J. He held four computer minidiscs in his hands.

"Gentlemen and Sue," C. J. announced. "This is Denny Zucarro. Denny will be supervising all aspects of the Junior Rocket Rally."

"Yes, yes, hello," Denny said nearly under his breath, bobbing his head. He didn't even try to make eye contact with us. If he wasn't an extremely antisocial tech-head, then he was a very good actor. In a dirty lab coat, chinos with high cuffs, and a cheap, rayon, blue button-down shirt, he seemed to have the part down pat. Something about the way he furrowed his brow and kept nodding made me think he was a bit strange. Knowing that he was going to be calling the shots from the ground regarding technical regulations for the pilots in the air didn't give me a lot of confidence. I shook off the feeling. Inventions are my strong suit. But when it comes to reading people, I have to admit that Bud is a lot better at it than me. I made a mental note to ask him later.

"These disks have your flight paths—your *skylanes*—clearly delineated," he said, handing out the information. As I took mine, I noticed that it was still warm from his sweaty hands. I put the minidisc in my pocket.

"Pilots," C. J. began, "I don't want to keep you from your rocket racers any longer. I'm sure you want to do some last-minute adjustments before time trials. But I do want to remind you that we'll be allowing the public in during the next two days to help generate a little more publicity. The time trial schedule will be posted at the gate when you leave. Thank you and good luck to all of you."

With that, she strode off, Denny Zucarro trailing behind her.

"Tom Swift," I heard over my shoulder. Turning, I saw an outstretched hand and a wide smile.

"Karim!" I said. I recognized him immediately from the picture that C. J. had distributed to the press corp. There was something in his smile that put me instantly at ease. I smiled and shook his hand. He is a few inches taller than me and well built. With his dark hair swept back and oiled, and prominent nose jutting out beneath his thick eyebrows, he cuts an impressive picture. What little I know about him I'd found on a web page for Middle Eastern pilots. He was an Arabian prince, very wealthy, and had been flying his father's private jet for a number of years.

"I've read an article about you on the Internet," I said.

"And I've read a lot about you everywhere," he replied with a grin.

"Did you see the article on Tom in the *International Tech Week Review* a couple of weeks ago?" Sue Itami asked, joining us. I hadn't seen Sue since the Robot Olympics, although we had e-mailed each other upward of twice a day since we'd learned we were going to be competing in the rally. I was glad that she'd been able to bring her rocket racer all the way from Japan.

"Nanotechnology breakthrough," Karim said. "Page A-1. Impressive work! I would like very much to discuss it with you."

"Now *that* sounds like a good time!" Andy

Foger interrupted, his voice heavy with sarcasm. "Nanotechnology, something small and insignificant. Just like you, Swift!" He burst into mock laughter, but without his friends/lackeys around to join him, his laughs faded away.

"Always a pleasure, Andy," I mumbled under my breath.

If you can imagine what a shaved orangutan with baggy rapper pants, a loud Hawaiian shirt, and a baseball cap turned around might look like, you've pictured Andy Foger. As obnoxious as he is nasty, Andy gives inventors a bad name. As the son of Randall Foger, CEO of the Foger Utility Group, Andy uses every invention put out by his father's company to further his own selfish desires. And he is not above stealing ideas that originated in Swift Enterprises' laboratories before they hit the market, copying them and putting them out as his own.

"I see you've brought the UN with you," he sneered, sizing up Karim and Sue. I could tell from their expressions that they, too, took an instant dislike to Andy. Smart, I thought.

Karim, being an obvious gentleman, said nothing. Sue, being a perfect lady, rushed to fill the void in the conversation left by Andy's barb. With a light tone and a smile, she changed the subject. "Karim, the last time Tom and I met, he bested me. I don't intend to be so kind this time."

Both Karim and I laughed, but Andy glared. The only thing he hates more than being beaten is being ignored.

"Who cares?" Andy's pride flared up. "I'm gonna leave you all in the dust."

I was going to remind him that there isn't a lot of dust at three thousand feet, but then thought better of dignifying his outburst with a reply.

"Planning on cheating again, like at the Robot Olympics?" Sue said with an icy smile.

Andy gritted his teeth and said nothing. She had him dead to rights. His eyes narrowed to slits as he drew the back of his hand across his lips. I'd seen him do that before when he was really angry. I never thought that he would strike a girl, but the look in his eyes told me he was pretty closing to doing that very thing.

"I didn't cheat," he finally spat out.

"Well, even *you* wouldn't dare in front of all the spectators who are going to be here," Sue finished.

"Yeah," he said before he walking away, "imagine how many people would show up to watch a Junior Rocket Rally crash. Now that *would* get some publicity."

Karim, Sue, and I exchanged puzzled glances.

3

Getting off the Ground

Though Andy's talk the previous day of crashing was bugging me, by the time I reached the airfield with my pit crew, I was eager to hop into my Swift-Racer. It wasn't as hot as yesterday, and a cool, steady wind was blowing the air socks above the grandstands. While the time trials were open to the public, they weren't the real deal, so not many people had shown up yet.

Bud noticed me looking around.

"Don't worry about it, bro," he said. "They'll be packin' 'em in come race day."

"Yeah, I guess," I replied. I was not as interested in a crowd turning out to see me as I was worried about C. J. She needed a lot of people to turn out for the Rocket Rally so the sport could have a future.

My sister Sandy came racing up from behind.

"All right," she said. "Here's the order of the time trials. Andy Foger is first up today in the morning slot. Tom, you'll be going this afternoon."

"Good," Yolanda replied, nodding happily. "That way we'll have another day to tinker if there are any problems with the S-Racer."

"Sue Itami will be flying tomorrow morning," Sandy continued. "And Karim will fly last, tomorrow afternoon."

"Day after that is race day," Bud piped in.

"Great," I said confidently. "Let's get to the pit area and give the S-Racer the once-over."

Andy's rocket racer tore across the sky over the airfield. All of our aircrafts were of essentially the same design, but slight modifications were allowed. I could tell from the roar of Andy's engine that he had hot-rodded his racer so that it was all power, like a muscle car.

"Wow!" Sandy said. "Did you see that thing take off?"

"Yeah, it's painted like one of those old WWII warplanes. Those fangs he painted on the nose are pretty wild," Bud answered.

But we were all thinking the same thing: Could the S-Racer beat it?

"I dunno, Tom," Sandy replied half seriously to get me wired up. "Looks pretty fast."

"All muscle, no grace," I surmised, eyeing the Foger Utility Group's entry at the Junior Rocket Rally. "Just like Andy."

But the sight of his rocket racer was giving me reason to worry. Grace and finesse may not be needed here. Maybe brute force could win this race. I could tell by the color of his exhaust plume—orangey blue—that he was burning isopropyl alcohol at a pretty good clip.

As I shook off my thoughts, I noticed that Yolanda was giving me the eye. "I know that look," she said. "You're not losing nerve now, are you Tom?"

I cocked my head, put on my aviator glasses, and tossed off a lopsided grin.

"Lose *my* nerve?" I said coolly. "Hey, I'm Tom Swift."

The truth of the matter was that I didn't feel so swift later in the day at three thousand feet in the air with an engine coughing like an asthmatic at a cigar convention. I jiggled the makeshift knob on the dashboard panel, which controlled the reciprocator that allowed for a greater mix of liquid oxygen to be added to the fuel. The kick in the engine stopped. Great, now I could concentrate on flying.

I pumped the accelerator, giving the engine more fuel. The S-Racer sprinted out of its languid pace. I banked up, letting out a long plume of exhaust to thoroughly warm up the rockets. I did a 360-degree roll, then cut back and flew through the line of exhaust. The plane was responsive, and I was hoping the crew on the ground was watching.

"Hey, flyboy," Bud said, announcing his presence on the intercom. "How does she feel up there?"

"Wait a minute," I said. I flipped on the flight visuals that Denny Zucarro had given me. The GPS-configured skylane appeared in front of me, illuminated on my canopy above the dashboard. Here came my first turn. I took it wide.

Shhhhhhwisssssssshhhhhh!

"Yes!" I shouted out. "She's flying like a dream."

"Looks pretty sweet from down here," Bud said. "We can see you on the JumboTron screens they installed here on the ground. Do us a favor and turn on the cockpit camera so we can see the flight from your perspective."

"One cockpit cam, coming up," I responded, hitting a switch. "How's it look?"

"That's a great video feed—it looks like you have the entire sky to yourself."

"It looks like it now," I said. "But that's not the way it's going to feel day after tomorrow when we have the other racers jockeying for position. Hold on, Bud, I'm going into another turn." I moved the joystick to my left, cut the corner a bit too sharply, and my tail stabilizer quivered a bit. I felt the vibration in my hand.

"Yo."

Her voice came over the cockpit intercom loud and clear. "Yes, Tom?"

"I don't like the way the tail stabilizer took that last turn. Make a note to check on that when I get down on the ground," I told her. "Could we have miscalculated the airfoil design of the tail section?"

"Possible, but not likely," came her reply. "Run the S-Racer through a few more turns and let me know how it handles."

"Can do." I made a mental note that although Bud

and I refer to the Swift-Racer as a "she," Yolanda and Sandy refer to the plane as an "it." Maybe it is some kind of gender thing that I don't know about. Bud has always been better than I've been at explaining why females do or say certain things. He can be a doofus around girls, but he always seems to have the answers to my questions.

Another turn to the left and then a quick one to the right—I cut it even tighter, and again the tail wasn't as responsive as I'd have liked. The whole plane gave a little shudder.

I looked out both sides of the cockpit to make sure all of the plane was present and accounted for. Both wings were still on, unlike the way I left my virtual plane back in the simulator at the laboratory. Yolanda's voice again filled the cockpit.

"Tom, when we were running wind tunnel tests, were there any airfoil deviations regarding air pressure coming off the wings to the tail?"

"No chance," I responded, recalling the hours we spent at the Swift Enterprises wind tunnel facility determining the perfect shape of the racer's wings before constructing a model of what became the Swift-Racer. "Using Bernoulli's Principle, the wings are perfectly calibrated to produce enough lift by generating more air pressure underneath than above. The air extending off the trailing edge of the wings should dissipate before it comes into contact with the tail."

"How are the wings taking the turns?" Yo asked.

"Well, we're still in business," I replied. "Those last-minute modifications you made to the wing supports were great, Yo. I think the laminar flow projections improved lift without causing any loss of control, and when I'm in the straightaways the joystick is as steady as a compass pointing north. But this flight plan from Zucarro is a lot hairier than I expected."

"Hey," Bud broke in. "You still haven't told me what laminar flow is."

I took a hairpin turn at nearly full fuel burn, putting the S-Racer through its paces, kicking out the jams. Then the instrument panel went dead.

"Lights out!" I shouted over the intercom. "Lights out and getting wobbly!" What the heck was going on? My visual skytrack disappeared from its projection on the canopy window; every light on the instrument panel from the fuel gauge to the altimeter to the engine temperature went dark. The whole aircraft seemed to be in complete shutdown mode.

I was toggling the fuel supply switch to be sure the engine was still receiving fuel, when suddenly the joystick nearly leaped out of my hands. The S-Racer was bucking and I felt a sharp pain run up my forearm as I tried to gain control of the joystick.

Then, from out on the wing, I heard a wicked hiss and an explosion. I looked out the left side of the cockpit window and saw a gash the length of my arm was blown in the racer's metal skin.

Holy mole! One of the rockets was on fire! This was like a bad nightmare I seemed to keep having. First in the virtual simulator, now here.

"Tom, what's the matter?" It was Bud. "Your readings down here are completely haywire."

"Complete shutdown of the instrument panel," I shouted, scanning the dashboard for any sign of life from the racer. None.

"Bail out!" Yolanda shouted. "I repeat: Bail out!"

Not yet, I thought. I didn't put all this time into developing the S-Racer to have it crash to the earth into a million pieces. After all, the plane was still airborne.

"Tom," Yolanda called out again. "What are you waiting for?"

I yanked back on the joystick, and the nose of the racer jutted upward. I punched the fuel line button, effectively cutting off the fuel to the engine. If I stopped the fire by taking away its fuel source and at the same time exposed the engine to as much wind as possible, I might be able to regain control of my craft.

The fire on the wing flickered, then went out. Yes!

Just then gravity reminded me that I was three thousand feet in the air with little to no forward momentum. The S-Racer was falling. I had mere seconds to turn the S-Racer's engines back on, pump fuel back into them, and then get the plane under control before I got very well acquainted with the tarmac.

The nose of the racer dipped and pointed down, and in a millisecond the blue sky outside the glass canopy was replaced by blacktop, grandstands, and dirt. Crunch time.

I hit the fuel line button again and tried to refire the engine. No dice.

"Tom." It was Sandy this time. "Get out of there right now. Right now!"

I don't listen to Sandy very often, but this time I

knew she was right. I was trying to fly a coffin.

I punched the eject button. Nothing.

I punched it again. Ding-dong, no answer.

I punched it again and again and again.

"TOM!"

I shimmied down in my seat and kicked at the canopy. It flew open, and the cockpit filled with frigid air. I had forgotten what all mountain climbers know: The higher you are from sea level, the colder the air is. And the wind at three thousand feet was stinging due to my speed. If I hadn't been fully alert before, I was now. My goggles were pulled violently off my face and whipped behind me. This was the real deal. Although I'd done numerous fun jumps from airplanes with my dad, I'd never voluntarily jettisoned myself from a doomed ship before. I tried to run down the four-point checklist that I'd memorized for just such an event:

1. Be sure canopy is fully removed from cockpit. Check.
2. Open safety harness completely. Check.
3. Cross arms across chest. Check.
4. Number four? What was number four?

The ground was coming up a lot more quickly than I thought. Forget number four! With a vicious thrust, I forced myself out of the seat and into the blue.

I took a gulp of air and searched my flight vest for the rip cord. The Swift-Racer was falling at nearly the same rate as I was, not ten yards away from me. I had the strangest sensation as I watched it fall. It was as though I were standing onshore watching a boat capsize and sink underwater.

And I suddenly remembered number four! I found the plastic handle on my vest over my heart and yanked at the rip cord. With a quick snap, my parasail opened and slowed my descent. I watched the Swift-racer twist in agony as it made its way to earth, plowing nose-first into the tarmac. I saw an explosion and a plume of smoke. Then I realized I was now a pilot without an aircraft. That meant I was out of the race.

As they hosed the S-Racer down, I stood nearby, too dejected to say anything to my crew. Out of respect, they were quiet also. We just stood there as the smoke from the wreckage meandered away.

Thankfully no spectators were hurt, but without a doubt, the S-Racer was trashed beyond repair.

"Tough luck, Swift," Andy said over my shoulder. I could tell from his sarcastic tone that he wasn't even pretending not to gloat.

I didn't trust myself to turn around. One of us wouldn't be left standing if I did.

4

Sabotage?

By nightfall I had gotten over the disappointment of the Swift-Racer's destruction and was more intent on figuring out why it had crashed. We'd had the wreck brought to one of the old hangars at the airfield and had started to go over it more closely. The polycarbonate skin that we had applied to decrease air drag had peeled away, burnt and loose, from the metal body.

"Foger did it, didn't he?" Yolanda asked, her voice bitter. She had put in almost as much time as I had on the S-Racer. She was the one who ran the wires throughout the craft, wrote the script for the computer program that perfected the wing alignment, and sat with me as I ran wind tunnel test after wind tunnel test. Yo was there every step of the way.

"We don't know that," I replied. But I had my suspicions.

The wreck had cooled off, so we were able to touch the twisted metal. I grabbed the remnant of the left wing and tried to shake it from the fuselage. But I only succeeded in getting my hands covered with black soot and some bits of the asphalt that had imbedded themselves into the metal body when it crashed onto the tarmac.

"Let's call the cops," Bud broke in, running his fingers along the torn polycarbonate skin. It flaked off like the burnt crust of a piece of toast.

"And tell them what?" I countered. "I built a plane that is essentially a chair strapped to two rockets fed with highly volatile isopropyl-alcohol fuel. They won't wonder how it crashed so much as why it took so long."

Yolanda exhaled deeply. I could tell she was tired. She sat slumped on top of a red toolbox, staring at the bare concrete floor. It had been a long day for all of us.

"Even if we go over the wreck with a set of tweezers and a magnifying glass, we may never learn why it nose-dived," she said at last. "A hundred things could have gone wrong, from a bad fuel mixture to a poorly installed stabilizer to . . . pilot error."

This I hadn't expected from Yo. And I could tell she sensed it in the way I looked at her.

"Hang on, Tom," she said, holding up her hands, palms to me. "I *know* it wasn't pilot error, but causes of crashes like these are almost impossible to pin down. I'm just thinking out loud what an inspector might say."

"Well, something happened up there," Bud said with frustration.

"Yeah," I said. "But whatever it was started down on the ground."

"We've got video of the crash—not only from the perspective of the ground, but also the view from the cockpit," Sandy said. "Would we be able to tell anything if we synced that up with the technical data that we were receiving on the ground from the onboard computer?"

"It's worth a shot," I replied. Sandy's cell phone rang. She whipped it out of her jacket pocket and walked a few feet away so that she could hear the call.

"One problem," Yolanda said, drawing her knee

47

up to her chin. "We don't have a computer strong enough to coordinate a video feed with flight instrumentation data here. All I have is my Swift-tronics laptop. I've souped it up, but it still doesn't have enough RAM to handle all the data."

"All right," I said. "What about Q.U.I.P.?"

"Your supercomputer? What about it? It's all the way back in the lab. We don't have time to set up a satellite hookup of the video feed and sync it up with the information from your flight."

"We don't have to. Run a coaxial cable from the media room computer here at the airport to the computer on the Speedster and download the flight visuals. Send it via the wireless connection to Q.U.I.P. back to the laboratory as we drive home. I'll have Q.U.I.P. compress it, and have it ready to be synced up with the flight data you have on your laptop by the time we get back to the laboratory."

"Sounds like a plan," Yolanda said, leaping to the floor. "I'll run the cable. Shouldn't take a couple of minutes."

"Tom, that was Mom," Sandy said, walking toward

us. "Yolanda's mother just called to find out where she was. I think it's time to go home."

I kept the Speedster far below the speed limit as we drove home. Night had already fallen, and the road back from the airfield wasn't marked as well as it should be. I was enjoying the whir of the tires on the road and the crickets chirping in the maple trees we passed. The night air was cool and it helped me think.

Should I talk to C. J. and stop the race? What would be my explanation, a gut feeling I had? There was something good to be said for gut feelings, but an inventor learns to trust in hard facts as well. And C. J. would want hard facts before she called off something she had such a large stake in.

In the back of my mind I was also trying to shake out an unwanted thought: This crash didn't have anything to do with Andy Foger. I was beginning to think that this bore the fingerprints of TRB.

Swift Enterprises had crossed swords with The Road Back too many times to count, and every time we stopped their antitechnology terrorist activities, they always seemed to regroup and hit again. The FBI, Scotland Yard, and Interpol in Europe all confirmed the same fact: These were single-minded terrorists intent on returning the world to a time before technology, and they would use any means to achieve this end. Pure and simple, they were fanatics, and a life here or a life there meant little to them.

My hands were clenching the steering wheel so hard, they were beginning to ache. I was thinking too hard. I gazed over to see Bud crouched close to the computer in the glove compartment. His face was a bluish green against the black night sky.

"How do I upload the video information to Q.U.I.P. again?" Bud asked Yolanda, who was sitting in the backseat with Sandy.

She exhaled audibly. "Remind me again why you had to sit in the front?"

"Speedster rule number one," came Bud's reply. "Guys in front. Girls in back."

"Tom!"

"Hey," I said in protest. "Don't get me involved.

Bud is just making up the rules as he goes along."

Bud gave me a look. "Get yourself a new best friend, bro."

I just shrugged my shoulders. After today's crash, I was not in the mood to spar with Bud over something as trivial as who got to ride shotgun in the Speedster.

"Did you download the driver to make the video connection with Q.U.I.P.?" Yolanda asked Bud.

"Yeah, yeah. Did that."

"Just double-click on the executable, it'll do the rest."

"Done and done," Bud said, grabbing the laser-guided mouse.

"Tom?"

"Yeah, Yo?"

"I don't think I made a copy of the flight plan you got from Denny Zucarro," Yolanda said, moving forward in her seat so that I could hear her over the road noise.

"Why? Did you want to go over it?"

"I'm not sure," she responded. "You were having some problems with the S-Racer's tail. It wasn't responding accurately to your controls, right? Let's say that someone monkeyed with the tail mechanism. Not enough so that you couldn't fly, but enough so that it'd cause you a problem or two in flight. A recalcitrant tailpiece could put enough strain on the engine to make it explode, or certainly shut down. What if Zucarro made the turns tighter than they should have been to increase the pressure on the rest of the plane?"

"I don't think that was the problem," I countered. "Yeah, the craft was difficult to control, but not impossible. Certainly not enough to cause the engine to burst into flames."

"I know that," she said. "But if someone was out to get you and they wanted to cover their tracks, why not throw up a red herring?"

"What's a red fish got to do with this?" I asked.

"Red herring," Yolanda repeated. "Something that appears significant at the outset, but upon further reflection, turns out to be insignificant."

"Mystery writers use them all the time in crime novels to keep the reader guessing who the killer is," Bud chimed in.

"Let me get this straight," I said, rubbing my eyes.

I glanced down at the Speedster's speedometer and realized I was going ten miles over the speed limit. The last thing I needed today was a speeding ticket. I slowed down. "You think the trouble with the tail is just a red herring, and the real explanation lies elsewhere?"

"Sure, your engine was under some strain," Yolanda continued. "But come on, Tom. You and I designed it from scratch. It would have taken monsoon-force winds to put enough pressure on the firing mechanisms to make them overheat and explode the way we are supposed to think they did."

"You think the Swift-Racer's engine was sabotaged from the get-go?"

"I'd say it's a distinct possibility."

"When would somebody have done that? Someone has been watching the S-Racer every minute since we've been at the racetrack."

"Before that, then?" Yolanda asked. "Is that possible?"

My mind rushed back to the Swift-Racer sitting in the garage back home and Sandy's cat, Emma, coming in through the open door. But who knows where we live? I guess just about anybody who's read an article about my family or googled "Swift Enterprises." It's really no secret we live in Shopton.

I was just about to relate my suspicions to Yolanda when Bud raised his hand.

"Whadda ya know!" he exclaimed, his voice rising a pitch or two.

Yolanda grabbed the headrest on his seat and peered over his shoulder.

"It seems that Denny Zucarro isn't what he appears."

"What is he?" Yo asked, more than slightly curious.

"Back at the airfield I thought he looked a little familiar, so I decided to do some research on him."

"And?" I asked.

"I did a couple of searches on him and it seems as though Denny Zucarro and Cap'n Chaos are one in the same."

"No way!" Yo shouted.

"Uh-huh."

"Who's Cap'n Chaos?" I inquired. I'd heard that name somewhere. "A professional wrestler?"

"A professional hacker is more like it," Yo said. "He's the clown responsible for more than a dozen highly developed, ubersophisticated computer worms and viruses. To be fair, he was really good at what he did. If you consider shutting down the entire East Coast's air traffic for twenty-four hours being something worthwhile. Which I don't."

"He was *that* guy?" It was hard to believe that C. J.'s scrawny, unassuming assistant and Cap'n Chaos could be one and the same.

"This guy is bad news." Bud exhaled as he leaned back against his seat. "If I remember correctly, he developed the computer virus called Slash and . . ."

"Burn." Yolanda finished his sentence. "It fried hard drives all over the world. Well, at least the ones that were unlucky enough to get infected. It took the authorities a year to bring a case against him, and then they almost didn't get a conviction because he erased his involvement so expertly. Eventually the FBI was able to trace down some old viruses he had created that were similar enough to Slash and Burn to convince a jury to convict him. He served some time in jail but was released a few years ago."

"Maybe he's putting his skills to better use now," I suggested.

"I doubt it," Yolanda shot back. "These guys don't change. The knowledge that they can destroy things, like supercomputers or people's lives, gives them a head rush. And they don't forget it. They keep coming back for another thrill and another thrill. And they're never satisfied."

"Who wants to give me odds that this joker is behind your plane crashing?" Bud asked.

"You're forgetting someone," Sandy chimed in, leaning forward.

"Who? Sue Itami?" I responded. "Forget it. I've known her since the Robot Olympics. I think I can vouch for her."

"That's not who I was talking about. What do we know about Karim al-Misri?"

Much as I was loath to admit it, Sandy was right. Sure, Karim seemed like a nice enough guy, but none of us had ever met him until today. How did he fit into this puzzle? Did he have anything to do with the crash of the S-Racer?

Sandy's question remained unanswered as we drove home through the darkness. No one spoke save for Bud, who told us he found next to nothing about Karim on the Internet.

5

Another Crash

Sue Itami was on her third lap when I noticed something was wrong.

No, nothing was amiss with her Manga-Racer. It was a beautiful rocket racer, done up like an anime butterfly—yellow and red, with a splash of blue on the wings. And the way it banked on the turns, gracefully lifting a wing like a ballerina raising her arm, was totally impressive. But something was wrong.

Sue wasn't giving it her all. She was holding back. She should have been testing her bird to the extreme, firing the afterburner on the straightaways to see how much it would take.

"Come on, Sue," I said aloud. "If you don't hit at least one-sixty, you can't qualify to race tomorrow."

And then I figured it out. She had been spooked by my crash.

Maybe fighter pilots during wartime were able to shake off the loss of a plane or a fellow pilot so they could complete their mission, but this was different. None of us, except perhaps Karim, were professional pilots, and so none of us were quite sure what to expect. If there was something nefarious going on, it was natural for Sue to be a bit nervous.

I had to give her credit, though. She hadn't backed out. Despite what happened to the Swift-Racer, she still had the guts to get up there.

Last lap. She was coming down soon.

I wrote one final note for her in my pad and stuck it in my back pocket. Sure, she had a pit crew to tell her how she did, but I was too antsy to just stand around and watch. Besides, I was rooting for her now that I wasn't suiting up to fly. I felt a little bummed knowing that I wouldn't be part of the rally after all the time I had put into my rocket racer, but I shook it off. It would have been counterproductive for Sue to see me in any way but upbeat when she landed.

She dropped her landing gear and manipulated

her flaps to slow her descent. Picture-perfect landing. Then all Hades broke loose.

As soon as her forward landing gear hit the ground, it crumpled like a tower of twigs. Sparks shot out as the metal bracers snapped off the bottom of her racer and got caught up in the right rear landing gear. They must have hit something significant, because the right rear tires exploded as the weight of the craft fell upon it. Instantaneously the left rear landing gear buckled and the whole rocket racer flopped onto its belly, leaving in its wake a curtain of sparks.

A siren! The fire crew was racing out to her.

I was already halfway to her plane, sprinting as fast as I could.

But Sue's plane didn't seem to be slowing down. In fact it seemed to be coming even faster.

And it was skidding almost directly at me! I realized that the plane had been knocked off its landing course by the crash. The speeding metal, sparks, and flames were drawing down on me.

I leaped blindly off the blacktop. On the side of the runway was a gully, designed to draw water off the tarmac. It was a concrete, open-faced pipe now littered with weeds and tin cans about a foot below the runway. I jumped into it and rolled over so that I was looking directly into the bright morning sun. In an instant Sue's plane skidded directly above me. Like a wall of fire it seemed to wash over me. I flipped over and plunged my head into the weeds, my hands over my head, facedown, getting as far away as I could from the intense heat.

The sound was enormous and awful, like some giant taking a steel building and sliding it down a hill full of rocks.

But in a moment it was over. The Manga-Racer slid off the blacktop. Its wing clipped the earth and the racer flipped once, twice, and then hit an earthen embankment engineered for this very purpose, to stop planes barreling down the runway uncontrollably.

I got up and raced in the direction of her aircraft. From the sound of the siren, the fire crew was still only halfway down the tarmac.

The heat of her plane was pretty intense, but I judged that I couldn't wait until her crew arrived. If she had any fuel left in the tank when she landed, there was no telling when it could ignite, torching the plane and everything with in a forty-foot radius. I plunged through the smoke, shielding my eyes from the heat of the scorched metal.

"Sue! Sue!" I yelled.

"Tom." Her reply was muffled, but she was alive.

"Sue, can you blow the canopy?" I shouted. I made out her face inside the cockpit.

"Hold on," she replied. She was surprisingly calm after what she just went through.

She took a deep breath before the canopy sprung open. Smart. She could see how dense the smoke was outside her cockpit and knew a breath could mean life or death if her harness malfunctioned and somehow trapped her inside.

I started to grab the hull of the craft to get a firm hold so that I could try to help her out, but my hand instinctively retracted from the heat.

"Don't touch a thing," I shouted. She nodded and punched the buckle in the middle of her harness, releasing her from her craft.

I reached out and grabbed her left arm, but as I did, her forearm seemed to go in two separate directions. It was like picking up a shopping bag where the bottom had just given way.

"Ahhhhh!" she cried out. Broken arm.

My eyes were tearing up terribly, and I was at the end of my breath. I leaned away as quickly as I could, filling my lungs with what was one part oxygen, one part isopropyl-alcohol fumes, and one part acrid smoke. I wanted to retch, but knew Sue would also soon be out of breath. I plunged back in.

"Give me your other arm," I shouted. She did. Even if this arm was broken too, I was going to yank it for all it was worth. The smell of the fuel convinced me that we had milliseconds to move, little more. She was able to stumble out of the cockpit, and I threw her to the grass.

She screamed again as she hit the ground. I felt terrible; that must have killed her arm, but I didn't have time to think more about it. I lifted her up by her waist, standing her on her feet.

"Can you run?" I shouted. The sirens were going mad. They must have been on the other side of the plane. If it weren't for a wall of smoke, we'd probably see them.

"I . . . I think . . ."

I didn't wait for her to finish her sentence. We half ran, half crawled up the embankment and flopped to the ground on the other side. Away from the awful-smelling smoke, we both took a deep breath and lay there waiting for the sound of her exploding plane.

"Tom, I could've been killed!" Sue was wide-eyed, her breathing ragged.

"No doubt," I said between breaths. The air felt sweet in my lungs. If I had had a few apprehensions about the Junior Rocket Rally before Sue's crash, now I felt full-blown fear. It's one thing to face death up in the air, but it's another to watch a friend go through it. It made things a lot more serious and put this rally into perspective. I was going to have the race called off.

"No doubt," I repeated.

6

In the Hanger

Sandy, Bud, and I stood around Sue's blackened Manga-Racer in the hangar where it had been towed to. Yolanda was lying beneath it, studying the twisted metal. Sue sat patiently as I opened the first-aid kit I had fetched from the Swift Speedster. My mom was a stickler for emergency preparation and so had made sure that all of the Swift family vehicles were equipped with the latest first-aid kits: protein-enhanced bandages, handheld laser scalpel, compressed oxygen canisters, and, my own invention: carbon nanotubes to heal broken bones.

"This sucks," Sue said finally as I filled a syringe.

I shot her a quizzical glance with a raised eyebrow.

"No, Tom," she said by way of an apology, "not your first aid. What happened to my racer."

"I know what you mean, Sue. But remember, it could be a lot worse. A *lot* worse."

"I suppose so." She hung her head. I couldn't see her brown eyes for the black bangs that fell over them like a thick curtain.

I drew the syringe out of the bottle, tapped it twice to get rid of any air bubbles, and moved it toward Sue.

"It won't hurt . . . ," I said as I injected her arm with the green solution, " . . . much."

"What are you putting into her?" Bud asked, wincing along with Sue as I removed the needle from her soot-blackened arm. I rested her arm gently on the table, careful not to add to the pain of her broken limb.

"Carbon nanotubes," Sue replied. "They make the ideal scaffold for the development of new bone tissue after a break or strain."

"Why don't you just wrap it up in a cast and be done with it?"

"Get with the twenty-first century, Bud," Sue said with a trace of sarcasm in her voice.

Bud was speechless for a moment. Both Yolanda

and I suppressed smiles. It was rare that Bud Barclay didn't have a snappy comeback.

Knowing Bud, he would want a full explanation of what I had developed in the Swift laboratories several months back. So I complied. "Bone tissue is a composite of hydroxyapatite crystals and collagen fibers that occur naturally in the body," I began. "It is exceedingly strong and would never break if it didn't encounter something stronger than itself, such as the metal found in Sue's Manga-Racer cockpit.

"I reasoned that if I could find something stronger than steel, I could do more than just heal a break. Essentially what I was looking for was a compound with a high mechanical strength, excellent flexibility, and low density. This would make bone stronger than it ever was."

"Okaaaaaaaaayyyyyy," Bud responded. "What's stronger than steel?"

"Diamonds," Sandy piped up. "Industrial diamonds."

"Right," I said. "They use industrial, or synthetic, diamonds to cut all sorts of things."

"You're injecting her arm with diamonds?" he asked.

"Not quite. I'd need a temperature of around five thousand degrees Fahrenheit to turn ordinary graphite into the highly refractive crystalline form of carbon we know as diamonds. Sue's hot, but not that hot."

Sue blushed. Sandy rolled her eyes. I continued.

"Single-walled carbon nanotubes are a naturally occurring form of carbon, like graphite or diamonds. And on the atomic scale, they are some of the strongest known materials in the world. At their *nano* level they resemble rolled-up tubes of chicken wire."

"So, you're injecting her with rolled-up chicken wire?" Bud continued his interrogation.

"The carbon nanotubes make an ideal scaffold for the growth of bone tissue, better than polymers or peptide fibers, as have been tried in the past," Sue piped in. "Once the nanotubes enter the body, they work in conjunction with the natural healing process by creating a 'fence' of sorts around the break."

I had to admit it: Sue Itami was pretty impressive. Not only because she had enough trust to allow me to use this fairly untested technology on her, but also because she remembered so much from the article she'd read about it.

"If I remember correctly," she continued, "you used several chemical groups to control the alignment and growth of the natural hydroxyapatite crystals."

"Calcium ions, specifically," I said. I was going to continue to explain the biocompatibility of nanotubes with hydroxyapatite crystals by increasing their solubility in water when Yo interrupted with a cough.

"Um, Professor? If I can interrupt your dissertation long enough, we have problems over here as well," Yolanda said, sliding out from beneath the Manga-Racer.

After Yolanda gave a detailed diagnosis of the damage Sue's racer sustained, a discernible pall fell about the hangar.

"It could be a lot worse," I said, trying to raise their spirits. Although how much worse, I didn't know. After only three time trials, we had already had two crashes. I had to bail out of mine, and Sue ended up with a broken left forearm—instant removal from the race. If something happened at Karim al-Misri's preliminaries, it could just be Andy Foger racing alone. He'd win by default . . . not at all a comforting thought.

"No, Tom," Sue said, her voice lower and streaked with sadness. "Like I said before, this sucks."

I finished my first aid by tying a cotton sling around her neck, and then eased her arm into it. She winced again and drew a deep breath. "I spent nearly three-quarters of a year developing and testing my rocket racer in Japan before having it shipped over here. And on my first flight in America, I crash and destroy it," she said.

"It's far from destroyed," Yolanda said, kneeling to once again inspect the undercarriage of the plane. "Your landing gear is as flat as old soda, but your stabilizers, rockets, and tanks are all intact, just a little black from the smoke. And fortunately your wings didn't receive any damage when you flipped. Just a little grass and dirt, but we can clean that off."

"What are you saying?" Sue asked, staring down at Yolanda.

"What I'm saying is that this bird can fly again."

"It's really just singed," added Bud. "A little paint here, slap on another polycarbonate skin . . ."

"We don't have *time* for paint and a new skin, Bud," Yolanda reprimanded him.

"Just kidding."

"What *do* we have time for?" Sandy asked.

"If we can weld a makeshift landing apparatus on it, blow the smoke out of the pistons, clear the fuel lines, put the canopy back on, and run a quick wind tunnel test on the wings, we'll be back in business," Yo concluded.

"How long will that take?" Sue inquired, excitement creeping into her voice.

"Forty-eight hours, tops."

"Let's do it," Sue said decisively.

"Hold on! Hold on!" I shouted. "There is no way I'm going to put the M-Racer back together just so we can tempt fate again. In case anyone hasn't been paying attention, three planes have gone up and only one has come down in one piece. When I was lying out on the embankment spitting out enough smoke to choke a horse, there was no doubt in my mind that I was going to get C. J. to call off the race. It's not worth it."

"Tom." Sue stood up and touched my shoulder with her right hand. "I was thinking the exact same thing as we lay out there waiting for my plane to blow. But as I was just sitting feeling miserable and you were explaining how you could actually make my arm stronger with carbon nanotubes, I was beginning to reconsider. You don't think that Andy or any terrorist group is smarter than you?"

"C'mon, Sue," I countered. "Nanotubes are one thing. Flying a rocket at three thousand feet is something else."

"No, Tom, you c'mon. So things look pretty bad. But if we give up, then all the work I put into my racer—no, all the work we put into *both* of our racers—will be wasted time. And if someone sabotaged my plane, I don't want them to get away with it. If I trusted you with fixing my arm, don't you think I would trust you with the Manga-Racer? After all, you're Tom Swift."

I raised my eyebrows as I mulled over what Sue had just said. There was a voice in the back of my mind screaming out a warning, but with everyone staring at me . . . I couldn't let them down. Everyone here had worked too hard to walk away now.

"Sue, you're right!" I said finally. "Sandy, get back to the laboratory and get in the virtual-reality flight simulator. Bud and I are going to stay here and get to work. Sue, your racer won't be as perfectly calibrated as before. We are going to have to reset a lot of figures in your original design. Pitch, roll, fuel draw, lift. All of this new information will need to be plugged into the simulator to reset the machine."

Sandy was already sprinting out the door.

"Call me on your cell when you get there," Yolanda shouted after her.

"All right," Bud said, "what do you want me to do?"

"First," Yolanda began, picking up a crescent wrench and rolling back a sleeve, "we need to get this racer up on a lift. Go find out if there is an operational lift in this facility. After that, I'm going to need your muscles. The bottom of the bird is pretty darn scorched. You're going to have to loosen a few nuts and bolts."

Bud gave a half salute and began to take off his jacket. "Aye-aye, Captain!"

I was more than impressed with the way Yo was taking charge. I never doubted her intelligence, but it was as though her natural leadership qualities were peeking out for the first time, taking center stage.

Sue brushed her black bangs out of her eyes with

her good hand and circled around the plane to get a glimpse of it from Yolanda's perspective.

"Wait, wait, hold on," I shouted, waving my hands above my head. "Wait just a moment. One big problem here, folks. Sue's arm is broken. Where are we going to find an experienced rocket racer pilot in less than two days?"

It was then that I noticed that everyone was staring at me, grinning.

I hate it when I'm the last to know something.

"So you think you can convince C. J. to let you fly Sue's airplane?" Bud asked me as we sprinted down the tarmac. Up ahead, C. J., Karim, and Andy were standing around Karim's rocket racer. He had just put his helmet on and was ascending the ladder to his cockpit.

"It's worth a shot," I said.

"Miss Garcia," Bud shouted. All three turned to face us as we slowed to a stop.

"Tom, Bud, how is Sue doing?" C. J. asked us.

"She's all right," Bud replied. "And so is her racer. Forty-eight hours and it'll be back in flying shape."

"Big deal," Andy interrupted. "She's out of the race. You can't fly with a broken arm."

"I'm afraid Andy's right," C. J. said. "Unless Tom invents a way to make bones heal overnight, I'm afraid it's down to just Andy and Karim. Although, quite frankly, Tom, I'm not sure I can go forward with the race. Two accidents in two days doesn't bode well. I don't want to admit it, but I'm thinking your plane might not have the kinks straightened out yet."

Now that my competitive spirit was up, this was the last thing I wanted to hear. Bud spoke up.

"Don't you see?" he said, raking his hands through his hair in exasperation. "Tom uses Sue's racer."

"No way!" Andy again. "No way is that going to happen. If Swift here can't control his airplane in a time trial, how is he going to keep someone else's plane from crashing into mine?"

"My plane was sabotaged," I shouted.

"Oh, yeah? Prove it."

"Gentlemen," C. J. intervened. "Calm down. There's nothing in the rules that says that one pilot can't substitute for another."

"Well, last I looked, the race is tomorrow," Andy threw back at her. "So unless her plane can be repaired in less than a day, it's just going to be Karim and me."

"Perhaps," Karim said as he descended the ladder. "May I pose a question, Miss Garcia? Could I put off my time trial until tomorrow afternoon? In light of the recent crashes, I would feel much safer if I were able to inspect my racer again before I flew."

C. J. frowned. "I don't know, Karim. I have a lot of money invested in the rally tomorrow."

"If you postpone it until the day after tomorrow, you might draw a bigger crowd. It will give the press one more day to report on the crashes. It's not a pretty thing, but accidents catch the public's attention," Karim added.

C. J. paused. It was evident that she was running through all her options before she replied. Finally she nodded.

"Karim, I think you're right. We might even draw a bigger crowd if it's held on a Sunday. I would hate to think that we would have to cancel the rally altogether, after all the work everyone has put into it. So, Karim, if after you inspect your plane you are confident enough to race, I think we can go forward."

Karim smiled widely. Andy scowled and stalked

off. He had been bested and was clearly not happy about it.

"It appears," Karim said, once Andy was out of earshot, "that I have made an enemy."

He smiled and I smiled along with him. I'd like to think that I had made a friend.

7

Suspects

The fluorescent lightbulbs that ran across the ceiling of the hangar swathed Sue Itami's damaged racer in a pale yellow glow. These weren't the best conditions in which to repair the aircraft, but with the race less than two days away, we didn't have time to haul it back to my laboratory. I also didn't want to bring it back to my garage before I installed security on the door. So as long as we kept some sort of surveillance on this hangar, we didn't need to be too worried.

"What time is it?" Yolanda asked, rolling out on a dolly from beneath the rocket racer.

"12:41," Q.U.I.P. answered her.

"Uh-huh," was all she replied before slipping back under, wrench in hand.

I guess I didn't have the same stamina Yo did,

because I let out a yawn. I had been sitting in the cockpit for nearly three hours already, tossing switches and checking anything Yolanda asked me to on the dashboard.

Sue sat cross-legged on the floor gazing at the mangled underbelly of her aircraft.

"Someone messed with my landing gear, I just know it," she insisted.

I twisted in the narrow seat to look at her. "I'm beginning to believe that myself," I said.

Bud's ears perked up at the sound of an exposé story I'm sure he was already researching on the computer. We had brought the Speedster inside and Bud had parked himself in the passenger seat, poring over the Internet.

"Andy Foger," he stated. "That's were my money is. You can almost smell how rotten that guy is. If anyone is capable of sabotage, it's that joker."

"Maybe," I said. "But I'm not about to accuse him without any proof. You remember what happened at the Robo Olympics?

Bud whistled. "Boy, did you have egg on your face that time. Andy was seriously peeved at you."

"Thanks for reminding me."

"What about Denny Zucarro?" Sue asked. "After all, he did have access to everybody's onboard computer."

"What's his motive?" Bud asked.

"Cap'n Chaos!" Yolanda answered him from underneath the racer. "Don't you remember? Anybody creepy enough to start a computer virus that shuts down the airport flight towers up and down the East Coast for a day is more than capable of sabotage."

"Yeah," Bud repeated, "but what's his motive?"

"He's a jerk?"

"Probably he is, Yo," I answered her. "But that doesn't mean he hasn't cleaned up his act since he went to jail."

"What about Karim?" The voice was Sandy's, coming over the intercom in the racer. I nearly forgot that she was still back in the laboratory running test flights on the virtual-reality simulator to help us determine how to reset the controls on Sue's flyer. Sandy can be a pain-in-the-neck little sister sometimes, but she never complains when there's work to be done.

"What about him, Sandy?" Bud answered her.

"What have you found out about him?"

"Well . . . ," Bud said as his fingers fly over the computer keyboard. "When I google his name, there are only a handful of sites that mention him. And only a couple in English."

"The others are in Arabic?" I asked.

"Yeah, but that's not the problem. I've got an interpreter program that can translate a number of different strains and dialects of Arabic, including the more popular ones like Berber, Farsi, Swahili, Urdu. But this dialect . . ." Bud shook his head in frustration.

Yolanda rolled out from underneath the racer again.

"Does anyone mind if I say what everyone else is thinking?"

"Go ahead, Yo," I said.

She lifted her head ever so slightly and stated, "Terrorists."

The room was silent.

"The Road Back?" I asked. Of course, I had thought about it before, but I didn't want to say it out loud—not without some proof. I was too scared of spooking the crew.

"Exactly," she answered. "You've been dealing

with these nuts for as long as I can remember."

"Yeah, but why would they show up here?" Bud asked. "We're just racing some planes. How could they be opposed to that?"

"Bud, they're opposed to everything involving technology that helps mankind in any way," Sue said.

"And I repeat: We're just racing some planes."

"Maybe," I interrupted. "And maybe auto racing is just cars going around a track. But if it weren't for races like the Indy 500, ordinary cars today wouldn't have Vulcanized rubber able to withstand speeds up to two hundred miles per hour. Or engine oils that wouldn't break down at high racing temperature speeds. Or antilock brake systems that—"

"Yeah, okay, I get the idea. But there's one name you haven't mentioned yet."

"Who's that?"

"C. J."

Bud was right. I was trying to think up a reason to discount her as a suspect. But she fit the description of a saboteur perfectly. Nobody would suspect her, and she *was* bound to profit from the media coverage of the two crashes. To put it plainly, crashes attract spectators. Spectators equal money. Enough spectators and C. J. might even make a profit.

"You know, Tom," Yolanda said, hesitation in her voice, as though she really didn't want to say what she was about to say. "The promise of a really spectacular crash would really draw a crowd."

"I don't know, I don't know," I said slowly. I didn't want to face this prospect, but it *was* a distinct possibility.

"There's one way to find out," Yo said after a moment.

"We can watch over either Andy's racer or Karim's tonight," I said, racing ahead in her thought process.

"If someone tries to break into the hangar where Andy's racer is being stored . . ."

"Then we know it's not Andy," Bud ended my sentence.

"And if we watch over Karim's . . ."

"Then we know it's not Karim."

"Yolanda, can you spare us for a few hours?" I asked.

"Sure, Sue can sit in for you."

"All right, Bud. Heads I watch Karim's hangar, tails you watch Andy's."

"Deal!" Bud shouted. But as I flipped the coin into the air, he realized the deal he'd just made wasn't so fair.

"Hey!"

8

A Shape in the Darkness

"How's everything look over at Andy's hangar?" I asked Bud via my Q.U.I.P.

"All's quiet," Bud whispered back through his cell phone. A pause. "What are we looking for again?"

"Anything suspicious."

"Well, I've been sitting here for two hours and the only things that look suspicious are two moths that appear to be doing a tango under a red fire alarm light."

"Why does that look suspicious?" I asked, more to pass the time than to get a real response.

"There were three moths here an hour ago," he said. "I'm beginning to suspect that one of the two killed the other one."

I stifled a laugh. Good old Bud. Dead tired and he's still cracking wise.

"When we're down to one, I'll call the cops. After all, they always get their moth."

"How are your night-vision goggles working, Bud?"

"Great, I guess," was Bud's response. "I remember last year when you were putting long nights into developing these instead of hangin' with your buds. So . . . why'd you bother?"

"What do you mean?"

"What I mean is, there are tons of different night-vision devices on the market. Why did Swift Enterprises develop their own line?"

"Improvement," I told him. "I thought we could tweak the existing technology, add a few improvements, and see if Swift Enterprises couldn't come up with something new."

"All right," Bud said. "*How* do they work?" Boy, he *was* getting bored. But so was I.

So I told him. "Night-vision goggles work by gathering existing ambient light like starlight and moonlight. Through the use of a photocathode tube the light photons are changed into electrons. The electrons are sped up and hurled against a phosphorus screen that changes the amplified electrons back into visible light that you see through your eyepiece. It looks green hued because that's the way the electrons appear to the naked eye."

"Sheeeesh!" Bud said, sounding exasperated. "I'm sorry I asked."

"Do you want to go back to staring at the moths, or have me continue?" I responded.

"Keep going," he said resignedly.

"The old units have a microchannel plate that works as an electronic amplifier. It was placed directly behind the photocathode tube to generate even more thousands of electrons to give a sharper picture."

"And?"

"Flip the switch on the side of your goggles, the one labeled 'GA.'"

I waited a moment before Bud's voice came back on over Q.U.I.P.'s built-in speaker.

"Hey!" He sounded impressed. "How'd you do that?"

"The reason you're seeing a brighter picture is because of a light-sensitive chemical called gallium arsenide. I introduced that into the Swift goggle to get an improvement in photoresponse. With that and an ion barrier, I was able to triple light resolution and lessen scintillation."

"Oh," he said with a chuckle. "Is that all?"

"Not really. After we developed the model you have, I realized that we could improve our night-vision goggles a smidgen more."

"Smidgen?"

"All right, a *little* more. I incorporated infrared illuminators in our most recent version. This means that if I were in complete darkness I would still be able to see. The goggles send out an infrared light that is near invisible to the naked eye. Whatever it senses, that image will be bounced back to the goggles."

"Like a bat flying at night using sonar?" Bud asked.

"Yeah, or like radar sending out a pulse and then gauging what's out there by the bounce-back response of the wave. I paired that with an electromagnetic wavelength shorter than radio waves but slightly longer than Terahertz radiation."

"What for?"

"To find heat. An object giving off heat is not always giving off light. Like a solid-state microwave gives off heat, but not any measurable light. A vacuum tube microwave would probably give off a small amount of light."

"A *smidgen?*"

I laughed. Then I noticed something strange on the roof of the hangar where Karim's plane was housed.

"Hold on, Bud," I whispered.

"What is it?"

"I dunno. Maybe nothing."

"Is Karim still there?"

"No, he and his head mechanic left about twenty minutes ago."

When they'd left, they were speaking Arabic and were too far away for me to use Q.U.I.P. as my interpreter. I had programmed it to be able to recognize over forty-five different languages and several subsets, such as Scottish, Brazilian Portuuese, Cajun, Jamaican, and Brooklynese. I figured they were just discussing the events of the day, but I'd have liked to have been sure.

"Do you want me to come over?"

"No," I whispered back. "Hang tight. It looks like something might be on the roof."

I flipped on the infrared sensor in my night-vision goggles. Adjusting for the hour of night and the light exposure from the lack of moonlight, I zeroed in on the roof. Nothing, really. A little movement—must have been a couple of birds.

"I think it's just a couple of birds."

"Tell me when there's only one left and I'll call the cops."

"Funny," I said, not amused. The hour and the darkness were starting to get to me.

"Tom?"

"Yeah, Bud?"

"I'm beginning to think we're on a fool's errand."

"Why do you say that, Bud?"

"Well, if I were gonna sabotage somebody's plane, I wouldn't wait to do it after two crashes," Bud began. "I would do it before anybody became suspicious."

"Good point."

"I would, you know, set up a booby-trapped computer program designed to go off right after the plane took flight."

"Do you think that's what happened to my plane?" I asked.

"Who knows," he replied. "But it would make sense. This way, after the crash you have no way of finding out who did it."

"Denny Zucarro?"

"I'm beginning to think so."

To be honest, my mind wasn't racing at top speed at that hour of the night. Too much squinting into the darkness had dulled my senses. Bud's reasoning made sense to me.

"Whadda you say we pack it in for the night and go talk to C. J. in the morning. Anyway, the battery on your cell phone is running low."

"The one you're using?"

"The one you gave me. Call me on my cell if you gotta reach me."

"All right," I responded. "See you back at the hangar. We can check in on how Yolanda and Sue are doing."

"Over and out!"

"Over and out," I answered, and began to stand up. Then I froze.

Something was moving down the side of the hangar, and it wasn't a pair of birds.

I squatted down and tried to get Bud back on the line. No answer. After I punched in his number again, Q.U.I.P. piped up to say, "Tom, he has turned off the phone you gave him."

Unfortunately Q.U.I.P. said it entirely too loudly. I thrust my wrist under my armpit, trying to muffle Q.U.I.P.'s voice.

Too late. Whatever, or whoever, it was turned in my direction. I saw eyes. And a body . . . but something was wrong with it.

It was as though two eyes were perched upon a wave running from head to foot.

A stealth suit! Designed to mimic a bird's wings, no doubt. We had been trying to develop something like this at Swift Enterprises for years, ever since my dad did work on the air force's Skunkwork project utilizing stealth flying technology.

Impressive.

The person turned away from me, and I was left watching the apparent ripple of a bird's feathers. The person wearing the suit didn't see me, or at least they saw me and didn't care if I was looking straight at them. Why? Because they were invisible to the naked eye. It was only because I was using my infrared goggles that I was able to make out any movement at all.

No doubt this stealth suit—any stealth suit, in fact—could disguise the body's natural heat: 98.6 degrees Fahrenheit. If you could "see" them without a thermal sensor, like the kind I had incorporated into my night-vision goggles, the suit would be practically worthless. But I guessed that whoever developed it must not have taken into account external heat.

Case in point: If you were standing next to a blast furnace with an open door, your body temperature wouldn't rise immediately, but the temperature of your clothes would.

And I guess that the heat of the hangar's metal roof, warm from the sun pounding on it all day, had caused the stealth suit to pick up some additional degrees—external warmth, unregulated by the suit's sensors, that took a while to shake off.

That was just a guess, a hypothesis, a conjuncture at best.

How did they get on the roof, though? Paraglide?

Maybe. We'd probably be able to find the saboteur's parachute in the morning. By that time, they'd be long gone.

Darn! I wished Bud would answer. I punched his number again.

The window of the hangar opened. By this point, the stealth suit must have cooled down, because I couldn't see anyone beneath the window pushing it open.

If I called security now, our Mr. Invisible might hear the noise and fly the coop unseen. If I sat there hoping Bud would stroll by, the saboteur might disappear back into the night.

I couldn't wait. I had to go in.

Keeping low, I began to make my way to the window. At the side of the building I waited a moment before I crawled in. I took the night-vision goggles off my eyes and perched them on the top of my head.

Then, as quietly as possible, I stepped up on a fifty-gallon drum and slipped through the window.

There was some movement in the darkness, but I couldn't see where; I could only hear the sound of sneakers on the hangar's concrete floor.

The noise stopped! Had I been seen?

Then I perceived the sound of walking again, closer to Karim's racer. Now whoever it was was picking something up off a metal tray. From the sound of the dull metallic click, it was probably something made of forged alloy steel, like a crescent wrench or a vise-grip. This was someone who knew their way around a tool set. If they were intent on simply destroying the racer, they would have picked up a hammer or a crowbar. This person knew exactly what to do, which was more than I could say for myself at the moment.

I waited until I heard the sound of metal on metal and moved again, this time hiding behind a forty-foot ladder leaning against the wall. I was pretty silent in my movements. From the sound of it, I hadn't yet been detected—the work on the rocket racer continued. I was grateful for this; now I was only about twenty feet from the racer. As softly as I could I began to draw in deep breaths of air to slow my heartbeat and get my nerves under control. I didn't have many aces up my sleeve and acting rashly would probably get me killed. I slowly reached inside my coat pocket and took out a canister the size of a skate board wheel.

I pulled the pin.

The working stopped.

I held my breath.

Outside the hangar, I'd say about two hundred yards toward the grandstand, I heard a sudden sound of trash cans crashing to the ground.

The intruder was spooked. I heard the sound of a dropped wrench, the rustle of sneakers across the floor.

I made a quick calculation and figured that in ten more steps whoever it was would be out the window.

With my free hand I grabbed the ladder and pushed it in the window's direction.

Direct hit! The top of the ladder fell precisely in the center of the pane, shattering the glass. There was a shout and I tossed my canister of Swift Stickygoo in the same direction. The can bounced off the wall and exploded in a mass of adhesive foam, rapidly expanding to cover the window, the floor below, and part of the wall.

But my cover was also blown, and no one was caught in the Stickygoo.

I sensed footsteps coming at me. I crossed my forearms in front of my night-vision goggles and waited.

Boom! A blow to my stomach. I fell to my knees and began to roll into a ball.

Boom! A kick to the top of my head.

I waited for the pain. But there was none, and I heard only the sound of my Swift night-vision goggles shattering. It hurt, but the goggles took most of the force of the blow. And then I heard the noise of someone breaking down the door. I peeked out from between my hands and saw that the door was being kicked *in*.

"Tom!"

It was Bud!

"Bud!" I shouted. "Someone in a stealth suit! Shut the door."

There was a flurry of movement as the intruder sprinted away from me. I grabbed another canister and pulled the pin.

"Light won't work," Bud shouted.

"Must've cut the power line on the roof. Watch yourself."

I heard the sound of a toolbox being picked up. The lid must have opened, because the tools scattered across the floor.

Crash! The window on the far side of the hangar shattered.

I lobbed my Stickygoo and a moment later a giant puff of the viscous goo exploded.

"Did you get them?" Bud shouted.

I didn't know. I heard the adhesive foam as it began to expand, probably covering the broken window, but there was no sound of anyone struggling to get free.

Then I heard a metal tool sliding across the concrete floor, and the sound of a person falling. I pounced.

I landed directly on the intruder. The broken night-vision goggles were ripped from my head as two hands scraped at my skull.

An elbow to my cheek. I instantly saw stars.

But it didn't matter. I had to keep this person from getting away. So wherever I felt him moving or trying to push or punch me off, I moved in the same direction.

Fingers in gloves tried to gouge out my eyes. The pain was terrible and I shook my head wildly, trying to get whoever it was to quit. That's when I found it.

The last canister of Stickygoo in my jacket pocket. I pulled the pin, put it between my chest and what felt like the other person's stomach, and locked my arms around the intruder.

I held on tight and a moment later . . . *pop!* The can exploded. It felt like being kicked by a mule. Instantly the goo began to envelop us both. I didn't let go until the force of the expanding foam forced us apart.

I guessed that it was about two minutes before I saw the flashlights in my face.

"Tom. It's Bud. Don't worry. It's security. I notified them."

"You notified them?" I said, spitting bits of foul tasting goo out of my mouth. "Who notified you?"

"Q.U.I.P. called me on *my* cell phone as I was

about halfway between Andy's hangar and Sue's. He said you were trying to reach me before."

"Cool," I said, exhaling.

The security guards had already pried the intruder from the goo and slapped cuffs on him. The stealth suit didn't work so well when covered in what looked like a tub of bubble gum.

"I would have been here sooner, but"—Bud laughed—"I kinda encountered a trash can on the way over."

"That was what spooked the intruder."

"Whatever works," he said.

"Well played." That was all the praise I could muster.

We both laughed as he began to help me dig my way out of the goo. I had never before been the recipient of a canister of this stuff, and now knew how well it worked. But as we scraped the adhesive off, I noticed the police heading out the door with the saboteur in tow. Even in the scant moonlight of the open door, I could see that the suspect was considerably shorter than the police. I knew instantly that at least it wasn't Andy.

"Hey! Where are you going?" I shouted.

"Sorry, boys," one of the policemen answered. "Ms. Garcia's orders. This has to be on the hush-hush."

Bud and I stared at each other. "Hush-hush?" we said simultaneously.

But security was out the door, and so was our saboteur.

9

The Road Back (To the Airport)

Bud bounded out of the police station. I was impressed at how lively he was despite the fact that we had each only gotten about three hours of sleep last night. Then again, he was always that way when working on a story. And the story of someone breaking into the hangar at night in a stealth suit to sabotage the rocket races was bound to be big—maybe even big enough to get him some recognition from one of the statewide newspapers.

That was why he dragged us out of bed so early, so we could be the first to learn the intruder's identify. Bud wanted the scoop and couldn't wait.

When he got to the curb, he noticed that Yolanda had moved up from the backseat to the passenger's side seat. She had been working on the computer

since the moment Bud went into the station nearly fifteen minutes ago.

"Hey!" Bud called out. "I called frontsies!"

Yolanda rolled her eyes. "What are you, six years old? Get in the back, Mr. Graceful."

"Tom!" he yelled, throwing his hands down at his sides. "Did you tell her about the garbage can?"

"I don't remember," I replied. "Hop in." The truth was that my mind was still a little fuzzy that morning. I suppose the excitement of the night before had worn me out a little more than I thought. I took another chug of Power It! soda and felt the caffeine kick in.

Bud jumped into the back of the Speedster next to my sleeping sister, and off we sped.

"Did you get his name?" I asked.

"The name of the intruder is"—Bud paused dramatically—"da-dum: Talitha McIntire."

The car was quiet.

"Who?" I asked.

"You mean you don't know?" Bud said.

"How would I know Tabitha McIntire?" I shot back.

"*Talitha,*" he repeated.

"All right, who is Talitha . . ."

"I don't know," Bud said sheepishly. "I was hoping you would. You usually have all the answers."

"'Talitha Ogert McIntire,'" Yo said, reading from the computer screen. "'Born: unknown. Country of birth: unknown. Profession: unknown.'"

"I guess you don't know who she is either," Bud cracked from the backseat.

"Talitha Ogert McIntire may or may not be her real name." Yo scrolled down the web page. "'Known aliases: Tricia Forks, Constance Ubanks, Drusella Van Meer, Janet Vachowski . . .'"

"Drusella?" Bud said as though spitting out a fly. "Who would pretend that their name was *Drusella?* Man!"

"Let's see," Yo continued. "She has been arrested in Bonn, London, Madrid, and Rome, every time for industrial espionage."

"Those are all the cities in Europe where Swift Enterprises has facilities. Either labs or warehouses," Sandy said, suddenly leaning forward. I guess she wasn't asleep after all. "Yo, where are you getting this information?"

"Interpol posts its most-wanted criminals on their website on a weekly basis. Talitha isn't in the top ten, but she isn't far down the list either."

"What's Interpol?" Sandy said.

"Kind of like an international version of the FBI," Bud answered. "What was she arrested for?"

"One guess."

"Antitechnology terrorism," I said. I glanced down at the clock on the dashboard of the Speedster: 7:30 a.m. I was eager to get to the hangar and check out the work Sue and Yo had done on the Manga-Racer the night before. I gave the Speedster a little more gas.

"Bull's-eye!" Yo shouted, snapping her fingers and pointing at the computer screen. "Ms. McIntire has been arrested over a dozen times, but never convicted of a crime. Although it says on the website that currently she is being tried in absentia . . ."

"Absentia?" Bud interjected. "Where's that?"

"Real funny," Yo shot back. "It means that her trial is going on even though she isn't . . ."

"There in the court or even in the country," Bud finished. "I know what 'in absentia' means."

"It goes on to say that she may have been employed by the Shopton-based company Foger Utility Group."

"Andy's dad's company!" Sandy said excitedly. "That means you can prove that Andy is behind the rocket racer crashes."

"'Fraid not, Sand," Bud said. "It makes him a possible suspect, but not much else."

"It still means he has to be watched, though, doesn't it?" she asked.

"Hey, if you can stand looking at him, the job is all yours."

"I didn't mean it that way," Sandy replied. "Did the police have all this information that Yolanda uncovered?"

"I don't think so," Bud answered.

"That's a good thought, Sandy," Yolanda said, clicking the mouse. "I'm going to e-mail them right now. Maybe this Talitha will talk and we'll find out either who she's working for, or working with."

"It'll never happen," I said.

"What do you mean?"

"These Roadies—terrorists in The Road Back—won't tell you squat. Sodium pentothal, scopolamine, sleep deprivation—nothing works. They work in incredibly small cells and always use aliases. They could be sitting next to their superior in a coffee shop and have no idea who the other person is. What little we know about them we know from a handful who have turned against the organization. A couple of years ago Swift Enterprises' Vice President and Chief Financial Officer Yvonne Williams was kidnapped when she was doing a routine tour of our labs in Asia."

"Hey, I didn't know about that," Sandy said.

"Mom and Dad didn't want you to worry," I replied. "One day she's crunching numbers on our operations in Singapore, next day we get an e-mail saying she's going to disappear forever if Swift Enterprises doesn't close down and go away."

"I hope they appreciate the irony of using computers to spread their antitechnology goals," Yolanda said.

"They'll use anything to further their twisted view of the world. They had a high-level computer programmer infiltrate Swift Enterprises one time. It took a team of twenty experts over three months to repair all the coding viruses he let loose in our systems."

"So what happened to Yvonne?" Bud asked.

"Long story short: She was snatched off a street

in Singapore and taken to some hidden location in the jungle, where one of her captors was bitten by an indigenous snake. Must've been poisonous, because he collapsed to the floor, he had a cardiac seizure, and his heart stopped beating. When the other guard tried to help him, Yvonne grabbed her pocketbook and pulled out her Blackberry. She took out the battery that she'd recently recharged and put it under the dead man's tongue. I guess there was enough juice in the battery to give the man enough of a shock to bring him back to life."

"Wow!" Sandy marveled.

"Yeah, great story," Bud agreed.

"So what happened?" Yolanda asked.

"The guy made a full recovery. He was up and eating in an hour's time. Later that night, Yvonne found that the room they put her in was unlocked, and that an old car was in the yard *with the keys in it*. She hightailed it out of the jungle and was back in America before twenty-four hours had passed."

"What happened to her captor?" Bud asked. "The one who let her get away."

"A few days later he showed up at a police station

in Singapore, scared out of his mind. They put him in a cell to keep him safe. He told the chief officer what little he knew about The Road Back, but all he really knew was that his time was limited. He kept repeating, 'They'll get me! They'll get me!'"

"Did they?"

"I don't know," I replied. "He disappeared. Maybe the terrorists got to him, maybe he changed his mind and went back."

Bud whistled one slow, low note.

I took the exit ramp off the highway and downshifted to take a turn onto the old road that lead out to the airfield.

"All right," I said as Bud and I approached Andy Foger from behind. He was polishing the nose of his rocket racer. The painted-on fangs were just about sparkling.

He had to have heard us coming, but he didn't even bother to turn around. More to the point, he probably knew what I was going to ask next.

"Who's Talitha McIntire?" I said with more than a trace of anger in my voice.

"I heard you had quite a night." Andy chuckled.

"Next time try fighting someone your own size—not a girl."

I let the insult pass. Bud pulled his pencil out from behind his ear and flipped his notebook open to an empty page.

"How did you know the saboteur was a female?" I said. "They only booked her a couple of hours ago and it was supposed to be hush-hush."

Andy took a swipe of carnauba wax from the tin he held in one hand and smeared it on his racer with a terry cloth towel.

"Had to be a girl," he replied loudly. "You couldn't beat a guy in a fight."

Bud shot me a glance.

"Interpol said FUG has hired her in the past."

"Listen, Swift, Foger Utility Group has employed over three thousand people worldwide in the last ten years," he says. "If she was employed by my father's company—and I'm not saying she was— how is that any of my business?"

I was steaming, not because of Andy's condescending tone of voice, but because he was right. We had nothing on him, and he knew it.

"Why is it that you are always innocent but

surrounded by guilty people?" I was trying to draw him out, hoping he would make a mistake.

"Just my luck," he said simply. "And your luck is to be surrounded by The Road Back."

"Who said anything about The Road Back?" I pressed.

He wasn't biting.

"Where would Batman be without Joker? Superman without Lex Luthor?"

I was boiling over at this point, but it was Bud who spoke up.

"C'mon, Andy. Do you really believe an anti-technology terrorist is going to have a stealth suit hanging around in her closet? Or that she would know the difference between a wrench and a ball-peen hammer? There are very few places in the world where she would be able to get a stealth suit and the knowledge of a rocket racer. And FUG is one of them!"

Andy very meticulously rubbed wax onto his racer's nose, a barely suppressed smirk on his face. He was no doubt thrilled that we were wasting our energy getting upset.

I was just about to tell him what I thought of him when he held up an index finger.

"Silence," was all he said. And then Karim's rocket racer tore down the runway past us. Darn it! I'd forgotten completely about Karim's time trial this morning. Had anyone even told him about the saboteur in his hangar last night?

When the racer gained some altitude and the noise wasn't too overwhelming, Andy started up.

"Tell me, Swift. In your eyes, will I be more guilty if his plane crashes or will you think I'm just saving something . . . interesting for the race?"

"What are you saying, Andy?"

"I guess what I'm saying is, watch your back." I didn't have to see his face to know that he was smirking.

"I think you'll end up watching Tom's back as he beats you in the race," Bud told Andy.

"Not likely." Again Andy loaded up his terry cloth towel with wax and slapped it on the metal tip of his plane.

"You should try to keep your nose as clean as your FUG racer."

This got Andy's attention. He turned slowly around.

"Listen up, *Butt* Barclay, boy reporter," he sneered.

"It's not *FUG*. It's pronounced 'Foger Utility Group.' Do I need to spell it out for you?"

"No thanks, Andy," Bud said as he put his pencil back behind his ear. "I think I got it: F-U . . ."

"Gee, that's funny," Andy said sourly.

And again Karim's racer flew overhead. In the drone of its rocket engines, Andy turned and walked off the tarmac.

I was still on the blacktop when Karim's aircraft came to a stop.

"How are you?" I shouted.

"Never felt better," Karim said as he removed his helmet. "Not a single problem. Whatever that saboteur was trying to do last night, she didn't succeed, thanks to you. And because I owe you my gratitude, I'm going to offer you my plane, the *Arabian Hawk*, to fly in the race tomorrow. And don't worry, I had it all checked out before I flew today."

I was taken aback by his generosity. This guy couldn't have been more opposite of Andy. I was also really relieved to learn that C. J. had filled him in on what had happened last night.

"Thanks, but no way," I said. "The people who'll be filling those grandstands tomorrow want a real race, not just a grudge match between Andy and me. Anyway, Sue's plane should be ready by the end of the day."

"I'm glad to hear that. I'm looking forward to beating the great Tom Swift," he said with a warm laugh.

I found myself laughing as well. His head mechanic took Karim's helmet from him and placed it in the cockpit. Then Karim and I walked off the runway.

"Have you heard anything more about the saboteur?" he asked as we entered the air-conditioned snack bar.

"Bud called the police about an hour ago. At that point she still hadn't spilled the beans regarding who she was working for."

"Do you suspect The Road Behind?" Karim asked.

"The Road *Back*," I corrected him. "Those wackos have been biting at Swift Enterprises' heels for so long that when the toaster doesn't work, I suspect them."

C. J. Garcia walked up to us holding a coffee cup, looking immensely relieved.

"Karim, your time trial was fantastic. You all set for tomorrow?"

"Good to go, as you Americans say."

"Great, how about you, Tom?"

"We'll be ready. Don't worry about Team Swift," I said with an optimism that was more an act than reality. To be honest, I wanted to grill C. J. as to why security had been so lax around all the hangars last night. And why had she hired Cap'n Chaos? Didn't she do any checking into his past?

I was getting *too* suspicious and I knew it. Doubts have a way of lingering in your mind and holding you back. I was not going to let that happen on race day.

But Andy's answers to my questions were too down pat. Too predictable. I even began to question Karim's honesty. Did he really not know that the terrorist group was called The Road Back? They're mentioned in almost every article written about Swift Enterprises. If he had read as much about me as he'd said, wouldn't he know that? But why would he be playing stupid? I didn't know, but something just wasn't right here.

I shook it off. If I spooked myself, I was never going to have the clearheadedness to beat Andy in the air tomorrow. And I *was* going to beat him.

10

Start Your Engines

"Here are your flight plans," Denny Zucarro said, passing out new minidiscs. "Don't deviate from your flight plans in any way whatsoever. We wouldn't want another crash, would we?"

I glanced over at Andy, but his face was expressionless. He took his minidisc, pocketed it, and walked out the conference room.

Karim took his disk and turned to me.

"Tom, is Sue Itami's rocket racer ready?"

"Yeah," I answered, "pretty much. We'd have liked to have run a few more tests on it, but what are you gonna do?"

Karim gave me a quick smile and headed out of the room after Andy.

Denny approached me and handed me my flight plan.

"Stay in your skylane," he said. It was more a command than a suggestion.

"Or what, *Cap'n Chaos?*" I answered.

He paused for a moment, and a flash of anger washed over his face. His eyes narrowed into slits.

"Or else," he said. And left the room.

I was starting to get a bad feeling in my stomach, and it wasn't prerace nerves.

The grandstands were packed. It seemed as though every penny of money that C. J. Garcia had invested had paid off. Parents brought families, and everyone had either a chili dog, soda, or pennant in his or her hands. Someone had started a "wave," and soon the entire grandstand was undulating. Rock music blared from the speakers. It was a typical summer day at a sporting event.

Red, white, and blue bunting festooned nearly every inch of the airfield. Wind socks stood at attention; a strong but steady breeze blew in over the mountains from the southwest. It was a little humid from the rain last night, but otherwise it would be a good day for racing.

Andy, Karim, and I sat in our planes, lined up on

the starting line. C. J. thought it would be a more dramatic way of starting the race than to have us take a couple of starting laps. I was impressed with the way Sue and Yolanda were able to clean up the canopy. I thought for sure we were going to have to construct another one after Sue had blown hers after the crash. Fortunately all it took was a little welding and glass cleaner.

I hit a few switches on the dashboard, and the instrument panel lit up. I tried to refamiliarize myself with the controls on the Manga-Racer. Some of the controls were labeled in Japanese and some in English. Last night I had taken the precaution of writing down the English translations next to the Japanese on masking tape. Sue must be left-handed. That's why all of the controls I was used to having at my right hand were now on my left. That shouldn't be a big deal. As long as I knew where the ejection button was, if I had problems, I could figure everything else out.

Her cockpit was a little cramped. It was designed for a girl, after all, and I guess I had about sixty pounds and a good half foot of height on her. But I wasn't here to be comfortable. I toggled the joystick.

It was a little bit looser than I'd remembered the Swift-Racer's to have been, but I was sure I'd get used to it quickly.

I gave my right wrist a tap. Q.U.I.P. lit up.

"Everything looks good, Q.U.I.P."

"Roger wilco!" replied Q.U.I.P. in his best West Virginia accent. I had programmed his voice to sound as close to flying legend Chuck Yeager's as possible. It was superstitious, perhaps, but I liked the idea of having one of the greatest fighter and test pilots along with me in the cockpit.

A red light suddenly flashed on the tarmac. That meant start your engines. We all did.

The light flashed yellow—rev your rockets. I flipped a switch on the dashboard, and a burst of bright orange flames shot out from my dual rockets. Karim's and Andy's machines also roared to life. Yet, despite the din, I could hear the even louder shouting from the grandstands. Everyone was ready for the race.

Green! The flames flashed out twenty feet, and our rockets shook. In a moment all three of our racers were sprinting down the runway. Andy got off the ground first, then Karim, and last me.

I drew my joystick back to gain as much altitude as possible in the quickest amount of time. My ears popped, and I dropped my visor down to shield my eyes from the sun and the other racers' orange flamed burners.

My skylane popped up on my cockpit canopy window. Blue triangles stretched out in front of me, showing me the way.

Andy took an early lead, firing his rockets quickly to get the tactical first position. Karim was playing it a little smarter. He was hanging back in second place, keeping his fuel in reserves, waiting for Andy to make a mistake, and then he would slip out in front.

I was starting to get a feel for Sue's Manga-Racer. It wasn't as powerful as my Swift-Racer was, but it was a lot more graceful. The stabilizers seemed to be working beautifully, the pistons were firing properly, and even the landing gear retracted as it was supposed to, thanks to Yolanda's tireless night of work.

"Great work, Yo," I said, flipping on the intercom radio. "If the gear didn't retract, I wouldn't have a snowball's chance of winning this race."

"Well, what are you waiting for?" came her reply.

She was right. I was holding back, a little fearful of hitting the afterburners.

"Here goes nothing, Q.U.I.P."

"Let's see what this doggy can do," came Q.U.I.P.'s West Virginia drawl.

I pressed the afterburner button, gave the engine some fuel, and she took off. The other two racers had already cleared the first turn ahead of me, so I hit it pretty strong, confident that the aircraft could maneuver well at top speed. I came out of the turn, flipped the Manga-Racer wing over wing, and sped up so that I was a near third.

Ahead, Andy put on another burst of speed. His burners lit up, and he dashed out in front of Karim. Andy was burning fuel at a pretty rapid clip. If I took a guess I would say that he'd have to take a pit stop pretty soon.

And sure enough, he dropped down to refuel. Here was my chance.

With enough velocity to overtake Karim, I passed under his rocket racer, carefully following in my skylane.

Shhhhhwwwwoshhhhhh!

His rockets weren't but a few feet above my canopy.

When he hit his booster, my whole plane shook. That was too close. I flipped on the intercom.

"Did you see that?" I growled.

"Yeah, that was pretty close," Yo answered.

"Do this," I said to Yo as I banked into another turn. Karim hit it tighter and was able to regain second position on my right. "Compare my flight plan with Karim's. Check and see if our skylanes cross anywhere."

Again I made a dash for second, dropping underneath Karim, and again my eyes were nearly blinded by the flash of his rockets.

"What's going on here?" I fumed.

By the time I wiped the glare from my eyes, I realized something was *really* wrong. One more near miss like that and Karim's afterburners would scorch my eyebrows.

"Tom, Tom." It was Karim breaking in over the intercom.

"Karim, did you see that?" I shouted.

"There's something wrong; we're flying too close together."

"Karim, I'm gonna take a pit stop and see if Yo and Bud have come up with a reason we're so close." I dipped my wings and began to descend. "Tell Andy to be careful as well."

"Can do, Tom," Karim said. "Hey, Tom, hurry up. I can't beat you if you're not in the race."

"Can do, Karim."

Just as I was landing, I could see Andy had already finished refueling and was halfway down the runway.

As my racer came to a standstill, I could tell that Yolanda had some news for me. She approached the rocket racer and rapped on the canopy. I didn't really have time to talk to her face-to-face, but I figured that if she didn't trust talking over the intercom, then I could take the time. I flipped off the intercom.

"Tom, Denny wouldn't let me have your and Karim's flight plans, so Sue and I had to run the original flight plans for you and me."

"What did you find out?"

"They're almost exactly alike."

"You're kidding!" I stopped to think. I didn't want to consider the consequences of what she was telling me. "You mean, someone was trying to make us crash?"

"Maybe."

"What do you mean, maybe?"

"Well," Yo began, "the paths never really cross. That would set off too many bells if anyone found out about them. They just go close enough to blind one or the other pilot. Once blinded by a rocket blast . . ."

"It's almost guaranteed that a mistake will be made," I finished Yolanda's sentence.

"It's a guarantee there'll be a crash."

I looked over my shoulder to see if Bud had finished refueling. He was just removing the hose from the tank when Sandy ran up to us.

"Tom," she shouted, joining Yolanda on the side of the racer. I had just begun to snap out of my flight harness. "Tom. We can't reach Andy *or* Karim on the intercom."

"Jammed?" I asked.

"Like nobody's business."

"Did you try other frequencies?"

"Jammed up and down the dial."

I began to buckle myself back in.

Yolanda grabbed me by the arm. "What are you doing?"

"Karim and Andy are in danger up there. I've got to get back up there and warn them."

"Right! We'll go pay Cap 'N Chaos a visit." She let go of my arm.

"Do you think it's Denny?" I asked.

"Who else?" Yo shot back.

"Better bring the cops," I said as the canopy came down.

"Be careful, Tom," Sue shouted as she and Yo backed away from the rocket. I punched the gas and began rapid acceleration. In a moment I was back in the air.

Andy and Karim had just taken a turn on the near side of the air course and were heading into a straightaway. They lit up their rockets at the same time. Twenty-foot flames shot out behind each of them. I would have to move pretty fast to catch up with them. Winning the race was no longer at the forefront of my mind, saving their lives was, so I really didn't care how much fuel I burned. My afterburners fired up. The force momentarily pressed my head back against the seat cushion.

I reached out and toggled the intercom switch.

"Yolanda, Bud, Sue," I said. "Come in. Yolanda,

Bud, Sue. I repeat: Come in. Do you read me?"

"Yer outta luck, son." Chuck Yeager again. "That intercom is jammed tighter than a heifer in a calf's stall."

"What?"

"What, what, sir?" Q.U.I.P. replied.

"Knock it off, Q.U.I.P.," I shouted.

"Sorry, Tom." His voice was back to normal. "What can I do for you?"

Karim and Andy were heading toward the far side of the course.

"Q.U.I.P., I need you to test the radio frequencies . . ."

"Like I said, all jammed."

"No, Q.U.I.P., not for audio signals."

"Then what for?"

"Each racer is sending a radio frequency to his pit crew regarding speed, fuel burn, engine speed . . ."

"Yes, and . . . ?"

"If you can communicate with those frequencies, you might be able to warn them of the danger their planes are in."

"Roger wilco!" Q.U.I.P. said in the affirmative. "Shutting down momentarily to access frequencies."

"Shut up and do it!" I yelled.

Up ahead, Karim passed so close to Andy that I thought for sure they were going to clip wings. One more pass like that and they were going to be playing "Taps" in the winner's circle. I gave my Manga-Racer all the fuel she had.

"Q.U.I.P.!" I shouted. I was almost regretting the fact that I had designed a built-in shut-down device into his processor to ignore voice commands if his circuits were busy processing other information.

"Q.U.I.P.!

"Sorry for the delay," his voice broke in.

"Tell me, quick."

Andy and Karim were banking again for another turn. Again I hit my afterburners. The whole ship was quivering from the added thrust.

"I was unable to achieve a dialogue with the other planes to give adequate warning. But I was able to download their flight plans."

"Beautiful, Q.U.I.P. Display them up on the canopy."

In an instant I saw Karim's red circles and Andy's maroon squares overlap my own blue triangle flight plans.

"Fast-forward their trajectories."

All three of the colored symbols flew rapidly across my windscreen until the point where they all met—at the same location. If it was Denny Zucarro who loaded these flight plans, then he intended to kill us all.

"If you slow down, Tom, you might be able to avoid being in the crash," Q.U.I.P. stated.

"No chance," I spat out. "Give her all she's got."

"Yes, sir!" my glorified PDA responded.

"Overload the engines if you have to, all ahead full!"

A moment passed while Q.U.I.P. conversed with the onboard computer, overriding the fail-safe that normally wouldn't allow such a dangerous engine burn.

Then the whole machine kicked like an angry mule. The joystick nearly leaped out of my hand.

"Q.U.I.P., engage backup stabilizers!"

But even that did little to smooth out the bumpy ride. It was a good thing that I'd spent so much time in the virtual-reality simulator, otherwise I'd be majorly panicking right now.

"Tom, we're dangerously low on fuel."

Up ahead I watched as Andy's plane flew perfectly in his maroon square flight trajectory on my windshield. In an instant Karim's rocket flew perfectly into his. In less than several hundred yards I knew they were going to collide.

"Punch it!"

"We may not have enough."

"PUNCH IT!"

With what little energy Q.U.I.P. was able to eke out of that already overloaded system, the Manga-Racer dashed between Karim and Andy. At the last possible moment they both saw me and pulled back hard on their joysticks.

Instantaneously the words "DISQUALIFIED! PLEASE LAND YOUR CRAFT IMMEDIATELY!" were spelled out on my canopy window.

I exhaled.

"Good work, Q.U.I.P."

"Just doin' my job, Cap'n," came back the West Virginia twang. I laughed and it felt good.

I was able to signal to Andy and Karim to land their crafts, although they really had no choice. By forcing them from their skylanes, I effectively disqualified both of them both. Better than being dead, I thought.

Andy didn't seem to think so. After we had all deplaned he came at me full force with both fists up. Bud and Karim stepped in, each grabbing an arm.

"Swift, you idiot! How dare you make a fool of me in front of all of these people!" he shouted, wrestling to get free.

"Hey, Foger!" I replied. "Take a day off. Don't be a jerk your entire life."

His eyes nearly bugged out of his head.

"What did you say to me, Swift?"

"I said, use your brain. Do you think I just flew between you to win the race? I was instantly disqualified too."

I paused for a moment. Andy's eyes narrowed—a sign that his mind was engaged. It wasn't doing a lot of heavy lifting, but he was thinking.

"Somebody doctored our flight plans so that we would all crash."

"What are you talkin' about?" Andy said.

"He's right, Andy." C. J. Garcia said. Behind her

stood Yolanda, Sue, and Denny Zucarro. Denny's hands were held secure in a pair of police handcuffs. Three policemen walked behind him.

"While you were up there, Yolanda, Bud, and Sue notified me that something was wrong—the same thing that Tom figured out up in the cockpit," C. J. said.

"Tom, are you all right?" Yolanda interrupted, her face flush with worry.

"Yeah, fine, I guess." I took off my flight jacket.

"Well, you shouldn't be," Denny Zucarro spat out. After what I'd been through up there, I guess I shouldn't have been surprised at Denny's venomous tone, but I was taken aback.

"You all should be dead!" he continued. "And, Garcia, you should be on your way to jail, broke and criminally liable for three deaths."

"Denny," C. J. began in a voice sounding strained and tired, "what did I ever do to you except give you a job when no one else in the technology sector would employ an ex-con?"

"I didn't need your charity," he shouted back. "I'm smarter than all of you put together. C. J., you've been living off my brains for years."

"I thought we were a team, Denny." C. J. looked seriously hurt.

"If we were a team, then why did you always treat me like a flunky? Who thought up the Junior Rocket Rally?"

"You did, Denny. And I never took credit for your work. You were the brains, and I was the public face."

"Well, I should have been the person the press was interviewing and the one on TV, not you. So I rigged the race. It was going to be *the* disaster you were never going to be able to recover from."

"Denny," C. J. said, clearly striving to stay calm, "ninety-five percent of all of your ideas were just so . . . so *insane*. Someone had to sort through them to find the ones that seemed viable and could work. And more importantly, invest in them. Without my business sense, you would be just another ill-adjusted techie fielding customer support calls from video gamers."

Zucarro waved his cuffed hands quickly in front of his face, flicking away her words like irritating mosquitoes.

The police took the opportunity to grab him by

the shoulders and lead him off the tarmac.

"C. J.?"

"Yes, Tom?"

"One question. If Denny was responsible for trying to engineer a midair collision, who sabotaged Sue's landing gear and the Swift-Racer? Denny knew computers and programs, but he didn't seem like an engine jockey. Plus, why would he want to wreck the racers *before* the big race? It seems to me that a guy like that wants all the publicity he can get. And what about Talitha? Where does she fit in? Somebody had to tip her off as to which hangar Karim's plane was in."

"Talitha is in jail," C. J. said. "But for how long, I can't say. All we can really pin on her is breaking and entering. If she definitely is a member of The Road Back, then she'll probably have a lawyer get her released from jail and then just disappear."

Carmen turned to walk away and I noticed Andy was uncharacteristically silent. I decided to stay and have a few words with him.

"What do you mean, Andy didn't say anything?" Bud asked when I explained what had happened out on the tarmac.

"What did you want him to say?" I countered. "'Arrest me? I paid off Talitha McIntire to sabotage the rest of the racers'?"

"That would be a good start."

"Listen, we know that Denny Zucarro was one behind trying to get us to crash up there. That might be all we ever know. I'm sure Andy is involved somehow, but I don't think we're going to nail him this time."

"So what do we do?" Bud asked.

"We wait. He's going to slip up sometime. Don't worry, we'll be there when he does."

I slipped my hand through the arm of my flight jacket.

"Hey," Bud said. "What are you doing?"

"We do know one thing about Andy," I said by way of an explanation.

"What's that?"

I zipped up my jacket, put on my shades, and looked at the crowds still in their seats. The afternoon was drawing on and there was a discernible grumble coming from the stands. The people showed up today for a race, and I decided they weren't leaving until they got one.

"Andy Foger doesn't like to be called a chicken."

"What did you say to him?" Bud asked, a smile spreading across his face.

"I said that we owed the fans a race."

"And . . ."

"He said he wasn't going back up there because I was going to try to get him to crash again."

"And . . ." I realized this was Bud as reporter, always drawing out more information from people.

"I called him a chicken if he wouldn't face me in an all-out, sudden death, winner-take-all race."

"You didn't!"

"Did," I replied. "Now let's go beat the pants off that joker."

11

Up in the Air

The afternoon sun was moving steadily toward the Shopton mountains off in the distance. Already half of the grandstands were in shadow. The JumboTron video screen that the spectators could watch the race loomed even larger and brighter in the growing pall. The temperature had lowered, and the air was getting heavier with humidity.

The sound of an organ came over the loudspeakers.

"Charge!" the crowd yelled. It was a little hokey and perhaps not so appropriate, but it did the trick. The crowd was juiced.

I boarded the Manga-Racer and ran through a few prelims before I got the engines revving. Looking across the tarmac, I saw Sue Itami with her arm in a sling. I flashed her a thumbs-up. She shot back a glance that said, *You had better beat Andy with my rocket racer.*

I winked, saluted quickly, and got back to business.

Stabilizers: check.

Fuel gauge: check.

C. J.'s voice broke in over the intercom: "Karim, Tom, Andy, here are the rules: three laps around the course. That's all the fuel you'll have. You won't have any skylanes to keep to. Instead you will be racing around four GPS buoys in the sky. You will be notified visually when you are about to approach one. Turn too early and you're disqualified. Turn too late and you'll never catch up. First to the finish line wins. Agreed?"

"Agreed," we all said. Like before, we were all to take off simultaneously—no warm-up laps, no jockeying for position. This made it more exciting for the fans, no doubt, but it also made the finish more interesting. Since we weren't staggering starting times, the one who crossed the finish line first was the winner. No waiting for times of other racers.

"Good," C. J. said. And after a moment's pause: "Gentlemen, start your engines." I hit the ignition, toggled the switch to begin the flow of fuel, and began to warm up the plane.

The sound of the engines was pretty intense, but Andy made it more so. He began to rev up his rockets to an earsplitting thunder. No doubt he was trying to psych out Karim and me. I looked over. Karim was calmly facing forward, waiting for the command to go. Andy was glaring at me.

"When I give the word," C. J. continued, "I want you to go. Three."

I gave my racer a little more juice.

"Two."

Karim's racer jumped a little bit from the thrust of the rockets. But it was obvious he'd got his brakes on and was waiting for the full count. That didn't matter to Andy. He gunned his rockets and exploded from the starting line early.

"One. Go!"

I was sure either Karim or I could have complained about Andy getting a head start, but sudden death means sudden death. No one ever complained in a dogfight that the other pilot was being unfair. Those were fights to the finish. And so was this. To the finish line, that is.

Andy was off to an early lead as my plane left the ground. Karim was a few yards behind me and to my right. The Manga-Racer felt good. Whatever kinks it might have had were shaken out during the initial race. Yolanda's recalibration of the computer systems to take into account the damaged metal on the bottom of the aircraft was pitch perfect.

Karim snuck up on my side and attempted to pass, but we were just hitting the first turn and I took it tighter than he did. I retained my lead and gave the racer enough gas to maintain a healthy second place. I knew I couldn't hang back behind Andy for long, though. This race was too short to allow him to widen his lead so far that I couldn't catch him. I was determined to keep up with Andy, hitting my afterburners at the same time and matching him move for move until I sensed a chance to make a break. At the same time, I had to keep Karim behind me.

Second turn, then third. No one had broken out yet. We were all relatively tight.

Fourth turn. End of lap one.

Andy made a move. He gave his FUG racer enough power to put some distance between us. Karim saw the opportunity, dipped under my plane, and came out in front of me as we hit the first turn, second lap.

"What are you doing up there?" I heard Bud yell over the intercom.

"Watch your fuel burn," Yolanda added.

I didn't respond to either one. I concentrated on the race. One slipup, one mental mistake, and I'd end up the goat rather than the winner.

Second turn around the GPS buoy. I didn't like third place and I didn't like seeing Andy's and Karim's twenty-foot-long yellow-and-orange exhaust glow. I tried to gain some ground on Karim's right, but he saw me, made an aerial feint, and I was forced back.

Third turn. I made a feint to the inside. Karim countered by cutting the corner too sharp. Instead of safely making the turn, he overshot the turn radius and wound up on the outside of the track. Here was my chance. I gave my bird some juice and it responded.

Rooooooooowwwwwwwwllllll!

My rocket's roar was almost deafening. Music to my ears. I was back in second place, within striking distance of Andy as we hit the last turn of the second lap. But Andy hit his burners the exact same time that I did. I gained nothing on him. One more lap to go.

"Tom! Tom!" It was Karim's voice.

I flipped on my intercom.

"I'm losing power," he said.

Was this a trick? I wondered. Was he trying to make me turn around in my seat and lose focus?

"What's the matter?" I asked through gritted teeth, my eyes forward.

"I have to drop out of the race. It is my engine. It is used to racing above the Arabian Desert, not in this humid, cool climate. My accumulator isn't responding."

"Can you make it down safely?"

"I think so."

"Good luck," I said.

"Thanks, Tom." There was the click of him turning off his intercom. But a moment later it was back on. "Tom?"

"Yes, Karim?"

"Beat Andy Foger."

"Yes, Karim."

Andy and I hit the second turn of the last lap at roughly 150 miles per hour. It was crunch time. Andy made a dash for it, so I opened up my fuel lines and held on. With my rockets screaming behind me, I wrestled with the joystick to keep control of the Manga-Racer. Left, right, left, I made feints to pass Andy, but he saw each one and responded in kind, blocking me with his aircraft. He was not going to give me an opening.

"Tom!" Yo's voice boomed into the cockpit. "Do you realize how little fuel you have?"

I looked down to the dashboard. She was right. I had one last fuel burn left. After that I relied on vapors. But if I played this right, it would be enough.

I made a feint downward as though I was going to pass underneath Andy's plane. This was a dangerous move in that Andy would be blind to my position for a few seconds. In those few seconds, anything could happen—quite possibly a crash.

He took the bait and lowered his plane to counter me. That was my chance. I went for broke as we made the third turn. I hit a switch on the dashboard that allowed me to bypass the separate chamber in the engine designed to give the rocket a steady flow of fuel. This was built into the Swift-Racer and I made sure we incorporated it into the Manga-Racer when it was repaired and revamped. What I did essentially was dump all of my fuel into my engine. Raw power.

I gained terrific speed and lifted at the same time. I must have been 250 feet over Andy's racer and a good 100 feet in front, if I had guessed his position correctly. I took the final turn and headed toward the finish line. The Manga-Racer wasn't finished with its fuel burn yet and I made the turn with enough room to spare. It wasn't the best position to be in, but now that I was descending, I was able to pick up some speed from the turn.

"Tom!" It was Yo again. But the last thing I wanted to be told was that I was burning fuel too rapidly and that I'd never cross the finish line.

I watched the spedometer climb to 160 miles per hour, 165, 170, 175 miles per hour. I felt the joystick quivering in my hand. She was designed for 160 miles per hour *tops*. As I came down upon the FUG racer, I could see the near blue flame of Andy's engine rockets. He was going all out as well. And the faster I went, the narrower my vision became. I was no longer aware of the mountain range that flew past me to my left, and even the sky drained of color and the cockpit beneath me seemingly disappeared. This was the moment that fighter pilots refer to as the "Twilight Zone." It's a zone you get into where only you and the target you're chasing exist. Everything else fades into the ether.

Even sound stopped, although I became vaguely aware of a voice calling out to me. It could have been Bud's. It could have been Yolanda's telling me that I wouldn't make it after evaluating burn time for my fuel. Or maybe it was Q.U.I.P. telling me my engines were overheating, or that there was a malfunction with my pistons. But the only sensation I had was the cold, acidic taste like gun metal in my mouth. I recognized it as adrenaline pushed to the limit.

Andy edged out in front of me as we drove down the home stretch.

"Come on, Manga," I murmured, praying for milliseconds more fuel to make the finish line. "Come on!" I finally shouted.

And at the moment all my dashboard engine indicators lit up, Andy's racer disappeared behind me and I crossed the finish line first. Despite the roar of my engine, I could hear the crowd go wild as I made a pass overhead.

Sue Itami and I ascended the first-place riser together. Andy, still bitter from his loss, stood on the second-place level pouting, and Karim stood on the third.

"Congratulations," Karim said, genuinely happy for us.

"Thanks, Karim," Sue and I replied in tandem.

"So, Swift," Sue whispered as C. J. approached with the winner's garland. "How did you do it?"

"Do what?" I smiled back, playing dumb.

"How did you know he was going to choke in the final stretch?"

"Easy," I said as C. J. placed wreaths of garlands on both our heads. "Remember how Andy was gunning his engine at the starter's line to try to psych me out? Well, we all started out with the exact same amount of fuel. And I matched him move for move throughout the course, burning when he burned, gliding when he glided. So if I was on my last drop at the home stretch, he had to be bone dry."

"Pretty smart," she said, giving me a soft punch on the arm. The crowd roared.

"No doubt," I said confidently. "No doubt."